"Hayden." Daniel took my hand. Again I was surprised by the warmth of his touch and the spark it sent through me. "Even if I don't take you back to Wolford, your mate won't let you go through your first transformation alone."

Rolling my eyes, I scoffed. "Look, this is all moot. I don't even have a mate."

"Yes, you do. The elders chose one for you."

"They had no right—"

"They had every right. They're not going to condemn a girl to death. They've chosen mates before for others when a guy doesn't step forward."

In frustration I shook my head. "I won't accept him. They can't control everything." Then curiosity got the better of me. "So who'd they choose . . . to be my mate?"

He released my hand and touched my cheek, his eyes never straying from mine.

"Me."

OTHER BOOKS BY
RACHEL HAWTHORNE

The Boyfriend League

Caribbean Cruising

Island Girls (and Boys)

Labor of Love

Love on the Lifts

Snowed In

Suite Dreams

Thrill Ride

Dark Guardian #1:
Moonlight

Dark Guardian #2:
Full Moon

Dark Guardian #3:
Dark of the Moon

RACHEL HAWTHORNE

SHADOW OF THE MOON

A DARK GUARDIAN NOVEL

An Imprint of HarperCollinsPublishers

HarperTeen is an imprint of HarperCollins Publishers.

Dark Guardian: Shadow of the Moon
Copyright © 2010 by Jan L. Nowasky

Library of Congress Cataloging-in-Publication Data is available.
ISBN 978-0-06-196290-5 (pbk.)

Typography by Andrea Vandergrift
10 11 12 13 14   CG/RRDH   10 9 8 7 6 5 4 3 2 1

First Edition

For Anna Claire W.
A very special fan. May you always be a reader at heart.

PROLOGUE

Fear sliced through me, jolting me awake. I was bathed in sweat, trembling. Drawing in a breath was difficult. My chest was constricted tightly, painfully. The blood rushing between my ears almost drowned out the howling wind.

It was happening again. Worse than anything I'd ever experienced.

I'd been born with empathic abilities. When I was near other Shifters, I was bombarded with whatever emotions they were experiencing. If one was afraid, I felt his fear. If another was in love, I experienced her yearning, her desires. Anger burned through me, but I wasn't mad.

Embarrassment caused my cheeks to flush, even though I wasn't the one who was mortified. Assailed with so many Shifters' emotions was like living inside a constantly turning kaleidoscope, only the various colors were emotions. It made it difficult to know which ones were truly mine.

But I was immune to humans, or as we referred to them, Statics.

The elders—the wise men of our kind—had become my guardians after my parents' deaths. Recognizing my constant struggle with my *gift* and the difficulty I'd experience being around other Shifters, they'd sent me to a boarding school where all the students were Statics. I'd been safe there, lived a somewhat normal life. While in residence there, the only emotions I'd felt were my own.

But the elders had insisted that each winter and summer I return to Wolford, our secret gathering place hidden deep in a national forest. The elders thought short periods of exposure to the emotions of other Shifters would acclimate me to the empathic experience, would give me an opportunity to learn to shield myself when I didn't want to know what others were feeling or to embrace the sensations without letting them overpower me when that was to my advantage. Why I would ever welcome others' emotions was beyond me. It was such an invasion of privacy—theirs and mine. I'd never been comfortable with it.

Two weeks ago I'd arrived at Wolford. Families had come for the winter solstice last week. It was a time for gathering, for celebrating our existence. So many heightened emotions were swirling around. And even though most of them were happy and filled with gaiety, it could still be overwhelming.

The families had left a couple of days ago, but many of the Dark Guardians—the elite protectors of our kind and our hidden haven—had remained. School was out for the semester. My presence was partly a test, a challenge, an attempt to determine if I was yet ready to live among my own kind.

Based upon what I was now experiencing, the answer was a resounding no.

Never before had the emotions slammed into me with such stark intensity. Never had I known anyone to be this terrified. What in the hell was happening?

The unnerving panic refused to relinquish its hold, wouldn't let me clear my head enough to think rationally. Taking deep breaths, I tried to set up a shield between the emotions bombarding me and those that belonged solely to me. I brought forth pleasant images: butterflies and puppies and ice cream. A walk in the park during the spring—the image so vivid that I could almost smell the roses.

But nothing worked. I was caught in a cyclone of someone else's dark fears. I couldn't control any of them.

All I could do was experience them. Nothing, no one, could spare me from the horror I was subjected to.

Light from a full moon spilled in through my window. I scrambled out of bed and dropped to my knees, my legs weakened by another's terror. What was he—or she—afraid of? What was so frightening? I didn't know who the emotions belonged to. I only knew they were there. I could get a general sense of where they were coming from. The person was outside.

I shoved myself to my feet, lurched over to the window, and pressed my forehead to the cold glass. The bright white moon cast a silver glow over the snow-covered landscape. Someone was experiencing his first full moon. Justin. I remembered feeling his excitement and anticipation during dinner. It made sense that he was the one I was sensing.

Tonight he would be added to the ranks of those with the ability to shift into wolf form. The first time was supposed to be painful and terrifying—could even result in death. Although it hadn't, not for hundreds of years. In the past, a couple of times, I'd felt the emotions of someone going through his first shift.

But what Justin was experiencing was different. It wasn't natural. Something was wrong.

Without thought to the harsh elements outside, without grabbing a coat, I rushed into the hallway and ran toward the stairs, yelling at the top of my lungs, "Justin's in trouble! He needs help! Now!"

Doors banged open. I heard the pounding of footsteps. Several Dark Guardians overtook me, raced past me. Only half a dozen or so were here in the manor. The others were out patrolling, guarding our beloved lair. I was hit with a carousel of emotions from those surrounding me and edging past me: worry, concern, fear, eagerness for the hunt, willingness to do battle.

But above all the emotions, more intense than any of them, was Justin's. Because I'd been connected to him before the others' emotions joined his, I could still identify which sentiments were coming from him. I was homed in on him.

I barely remembered going through the manor. Suddenly I was outside, the cold snow biting into my bare feet. Snow flurries whipped around me. Clothes were scattered over the lawn, and I watched in amazement as the Dark Guardians, never breaking their running strides, shifted into wolf form—racing into the woods, the wind rustling their fur. All except for Brittany Reed. The only human among us. But she was in such great shape that she outdistanced me without effort.

Following in the wake of their tracks, I stumbled from the weight of Justin's fear and face-planted in the snow. Terror again sliced through me, paralyzing me—

And then nothing. Nothing at all coming from Justin.

No, no, no!

I could sense the others' growing fear, their anxiety. I knew they hadn't reached Justin yet, because they weren't feeling the deep grief that I was. I knew what we'd find when we met up with Justin. We were all too late.

I pushed myself to my feet and started running again. Emotions suddenly rioted through me: horror, disbelief, fury, anger, determination. Then I came upon the clearing. The moon, at its zenith, provided a perfect spotlight. I didn't want to think about how Justin may have initially welcomed it, how he might have felt the moonlight caressing his skin.

Now, in wolf form, he lay unmoving upon the clumped snow. Just beyond him was the most hideous beast I'd ever seen. I knew what it was. I knew what it had done. A harvester. With long talons, sharp teeth. Standing on two legs, looking grotesquely human, it towered over everyone. The Dark Guardians attacked it, their growls turning into yelps as they fell away, their mouths blistering from its unholy heat where they'd tried to tear into it and their sides bleeding where it had caught them with its talons or teeth. It was an otherworldly creature. At that moment, it seemed invincible.

"Enough!" The deep, commanding shout echoed

between the trees, shook snow from the branches. I glanced over and saw the three elders, all wearing long robes, standing there with Elder Wilde slightly in front. He'd been the one who'd given the order.

The wolves, their wounds healed, went low to the ground, ready to pounce again, teeth bared, low growls emitting from their throats. The creature ignored them as though they were merely stuffed toys. Then his gaze zeroed in on me and my heart galloped.

"Hayden Holland." The harvester wasn't human, but it still had the ability to speak, and its voice sounded as though it traveled through a wall of phlegm. It smelled of rotten eggs. "We will meet again during the next full moon."

"What are you? A writer for bad horror movies?" I didn't know where I'd found the bravado to speak. The snark was my need to demonstrate that it wouldn't dim my spirit, that I wouldn't go down easily, that like Justin, I would fight with every breath that remained in me.

It collapsed into a cloud of mist and slithered back through the trees, low to the ground, like a retreating snake. For that brief moment in time when it had been concentrating on me, I'd felt the fear and agony of a thousand souls: Shifters it had reaped and harvested.

In wolf form, all except for Brittany, the Dark Guardians circled Justin. I knew he was gone. That his soul was now one of those held by the harvester. Tears rolled down my cheeks, crystallized on my lashes. If only I'd recognized his fear sooner, could we have done more? Could we have saved him?

Brittany took a step back and when she was beside me, she whispered, "He died as a wolf. He should have reverted back to human form."

I nodded. He should have. But not when the creature we'd just seen had his way.

When I visited Wolford and dealing with others' emotions became too much, sometimes I'd sneak away to the treasures room, where the artifacts of our kind were kept and watched over by the elders. They indulged me. Had even allowed me to touch and read the ancient texts, had taught me how to decipher the ancient symbols. So I knew a little more about the harvester than she did apparently.

The harvester rose from the bowels of hell during a full moon to snatch the power and soul of a Shifter during the height of his transformation, leaving the body without the means to shift back into human form. It fed on fear and gathered strength from our abilities. There hadn't been a sighting in centuries. Some had begun to think the harvester was nothing except myth and legend. Unfortunately, they'd been wrong.

The forest was so quiet that I could have heard a pine needle drop.

Elder Thomas moved forward and knelt beside Justin. He buried his hand in Justin's fur. The elders were strong enough to shield their emotions from me, so I couldn't feel what he was feeling, but I knew it all the same. The overwhelming grief was etched clearly on his face. In spite of the fact that he was nearing one hundred, he cradled Justin in his arms, stood, and carried him toward the manor. The others followed. All except Elder Wilde, who approached me, his eyes a well of sadness.

"We'll ensure that you do not suffer the same fate," he said quietly.

And exactly how are you going to do that? I almost asked. But I'd been taught not to disrespect the elders.

As though knowing my thoughts, he dropped his hand heavily on my shoulder. Always I'd drawn comfort from his touch. Tonight I felt nothing.

"We'll research the ancient texts. We'll find a way to destroy it. It'll be all right, Hayden," Elder Wilde said to me as he guided me back toward the manor.

It wasn't reassuring to learn that he, the wisest of the wise, didn't know how to destroy the harvester. A month wasn't very long to search through old books for the answer.

Wolford was our haven, our sanctuary, but we'd been unable to protect Justin, to save him. The harvester had come for him. Next full moon, it would come for me.

Not only for me but for my mate.

While guys went through their first transformation alone, legend had it that girls required a mate to guide them through it in order to survive. Sexist, but there it was, a tradition begun way before women demanded equality. My latest presence at Wolford was also supposed to serve as my opportunity to secure a mate before my full moon. So far that quest had been a total bust. What guy in his right mind wanted to hang around with a girl who sensed everything he was feeling, who experienced it exactly as he did?

But I was no longer convinced that not having a mate was a bad thing. He would transform at the precise moment that I did. A special deal for the harvester. Two for the price of one.

I couldn't allow that to happen, couldn't risk another's life. Even if it meant sacrificing my own. I knew the elders and the Dark Guardians wouldn't approve of my plan. But I couldn't see that it was their decision to make.

I couldn't stay at Wolford. I had to escape. Tonight. I'd run fast and hard. I'd hide. Until the next full moon—

ONE

Almost three weeks later

"Here you go," I said, smiling brightly as I handed the cute guy at the counter his mug of hot apple cider.

"Thanks . . ." He leaned forward, read the name tag pinned to my red sweater, and winked. "Hayden."

I hadn't bothered with a fake name. It wouldn't have gained me anything. If the Dark Guardians were searching for me, they'd use my scent—not my name—to locate me. It was the reason that I hadn't changed the color or style of my sandy blond hair. I wore it pulled back when I was at work, but otherwise I left it to flow past my shoulders. No disguise would fool my kind. Even perfumes wouldn't cover up the essence of my true scent. And wolves with human minds were the best trackers in the world. I was taking the tactic that hiding in plain sight was my best defense. In truth, my only defense.

"You've got the most unusual eyes," he continued. "They remind me of caramel."

They *were* rather distinct. Not dark enough to be brown, not quite hazel. Caramel was as good a description as any. "Thanks," I said. He was cute but not really my type—being a full human and all.

"Where do you go to school?" he asked.

It was the most frequently asked question, quickly followed by what's your major, then do you have a boyfriend. My answer was always the same corny line that one of the other workers, Lisa, had suggested I use: If I told you, then I'd have to kill you. I hoped my flirty smile would soften the blow of brushing him off.

It must have worked. He didn't seem at all offended, because he laughed as I gave him change. But his next words alerted me that, unfortunately, he hadn't quite gotten the true message.

"Hey, come on," he cajoled. "Maybe we go to the same school."

Since I'd graduated midyear from an all-girls boarding school, I doubted it.

"Sorry," I lied, "but our boss docks our pay if we're caught flirting." He didn't. Spike was cool, but this was the quickest way to avoid getting caught in the flirtation net. I'd been in Athena for almost three weeks, and it was unlikely that I'd stay. I wasn't interested in a short-term relationship—and certainly not one with a Static. It could lead to nothing except trouble. Besides, my kind mated for life. We searched for the one and only, simply weren't drawn to the temporary. Due to my genetic makeup, I didn't find Statics all that sexy. They might look like us, but below the surface they were so plain. I peered around him. "Next."

Cute-stuff got the message and shouldered his way through the crowd, stopping to flirt with a girl who was waiting in line. I hoped he had more luck connecting with her. He seemed nice, but he just wasn't my type.

As a skinny guy took his place at the front of the line and lifted his gaze to the menu posted on the wall behind me, I refrained from rolling my eyes. Things would move so much more quickly if people used their time in line to study the menu and decide what they wanted *before* they got to me. But most stood there talking about the awesome slopes or powder or tomorrow's forecast.

Business was always brisk at twilight, as the sun descended beyond the snow-covered mountains, forcing the skiers to abandon the slopes. People crowded the front of the counter, trying to get their hot beverages—coffee, chocolate, tea, cider—to warm themselves. The din of their laughter and voices drowned out our snow tunes playlist, which repeated constantly to remind people how cold it was outside and tempt them into ordering the Bigfoot-sized mugs. I relished the fact that all these people didn't bother me. They almost filled me with a sense of calm, because I couldn't *feel* their deepest fears or yearnings. The only emotions cascading through me were mine.

The door opened, just as it had dozens of times that day, but for some reason, this time it drew my attention. Drew everyone's, as there was a collective holding of breath for just a heartbeat before the din started again. It wasn't the door so much as the guy striding through it. Tall, dark, and handsome was a cliché, but it fit him perfectly. My heart stuttered. I recognized him immediately.

Daniel Foster. A Shifter. A Dark Guardian.

Crap. What the hell was he doing here?

Until he'd walked in, I hadn't been aware of any Shifters in the area. It bothered me that I hadn't known he was at the resort until I saw him. I'd never tested the full limits of my ability, but I knew I could easily sense a Shifter's emotions if he was within a block or so of where I was. If his emotions were ratcheted up to the extreme like Justin's had been the night he died, I could sense him farther away than that. So I should have felt Daniel's presence before he strode through that door. I should have known he was nearby so I could have run. Why had he taken me by surprise? Did he have the ability to shut down his emotions? Even now that I could see him, I couldn't tap into what he was feeling. I was as bothered by that fact as I was by his presence—which I was fairly certain didn't bode well for me.

I didn't know much about Daniel. He'd joined our pack only last summer. I'd seen him a couple of times from a distance when I'd visited Wolford last June. But I hadn't paid a great deal of attention to him. I figured he could have his choice of mate, and I'd never been on any Shifter's Girl Most Likely to Be Asked Out list.

He wore a black, quilted down jacket that he hadn't bothered to zip, so his dark-gray sweater beneath it was visible. His black hair was cropped short. His facial features were rugged, chiseled as though they'd been carved from the roughest granite. In the middle of winter he was deeply tanned—like any self-respecting guy who lived for the outdoors. The stubble shadowing his strong jaw gave him a dangerous edge.

Other guys hanging around in the Hot Brew Café were unshaven, too. Athena was one of the most popular winter vacation resorts in the state, and few people dressed up for it. But none of them looked as though they had the ability—or desire—to defend their territory. Daniel gave off the aura that he marked it and would willingly take down anyone who crossed the line into what he considered his. He was not someone to mess with.

Even his eyes—the most amazing, mesmerizing green, like emeralds—were those of a competent hunter. He simply stood there, his well-toned body so still, so very still, the way a predator waits for the precise moment to pounce on its prey. His only movement was his gaze slowly scanning the shop. Then it locked with mine and I was hit with a quivering sense of dread.

Within his eyes, I saw recognition and triumph—but I didn't *feel* them. But more important, I realized *I* was his prey. Just as I'd feared, *I* was the reason he was here.

He ambled over to the far end of the counter where there were stools—all occupied. He came to a stop behind the one in the corner. The buff guy sitting on it gave a little startled jump as though someone had given him a wedgie. He glanced back over his shoulder at Daniel, then grabbed his coffee cup and slunk away. Daniel's power of intimidation without confrontation was incredible, but deeply unsettling because I still couldn't tap into his emotions—even with his increasing nearness. I should have felt *something*.

I forced myself to break the spell, to snap my attention away from Daniel and back to the guy who'd been studying the menu. After taking his order, I turned to the preparation counter, where we kept all the essentials for the beverages we provided. I focused on my task. Two scoops of chocolate powder. A dab of marshmallow cream. Hot water from the spigot. Stir briskly. I watched the contents swirling, melting. *Focus. Focus. Don't look around. Don't let him know you're aware that he's watching you.*

But I *was* acutely aware of him watching me, the way an animal in the forest knows it's been targeted. The hairs on the nape of my neck prickled and rose, sending an icy shimmer skittering along my spine. I handed the mug of chocolate to the customer and took his money.

In spite of my best efforts not to, I slid my gaze to the side. Daniel sat unmoving, his eyes lasering in on me. He was the storm, the thunder and lightning that turned the blue sky to gray. Not literally, of course. Metaphorically. But if ever there was a guy who emanated danger, he was it.

"Hey, Hayden—"

I nearly jumped out of my skin when Lisa placed her hand lightly on my shoulder. Her short-cropped black hair stood at various angles as if she'd just crawled out of bed. Black kohl lined her cobalt-blue eyes. She had a diamond stud in the side of her nose. I'd pegged her as harsh and radical when I'd first met her. But she was actually sweet and fun. The closest thing I had to a friend. Best of all, like everyone else here, she kept her emotions to herself.

"I noticed you and hot guy seemed to connect," she said. "I'll handle the to-go orders if you want to wait on him."

Lisa had been taking care of the customers who were seated at the counter and at tables. I took an order for a mint chocolate and a mint chocolate mocha from a tall guy who had his arm slung around a short girl's shoulders. Even before I turned to the preparation area to begin mixing the drinks, he'd planted his lips on hers.

"That's okay, I'm busy here," I muttered to Lisa.

Her eyes widened as though she thought I was a total loser not to jump at this opportunity. "Did you not see the way he looked at you? And he is apparently alone. *Hello?* This might be your chance to do something besides curl up with a book at night."

I *liked* curling up with a good book. Lisa tended to curl up with any available guy after work.

"I don't want to break my routine," I said, working to keep my voice flat. I turned the milk frother on, focusing on my work, and trying to drown out Lisa's cajoling. I took a deep breath, confused by my own feelings. I was slightly grateful to know the elders cared enough to send someone to find me and bothered by the fact that he'd succeeded in finding me. Panic made my voice want to warble. I hated it. With the milk sufficiently frothy, I shut off the machine. "If you want him, go for it," I told Lisa.

"Seriously?"

"Sure."

She grinned, her blue eyes sparkling. She bounced as though she had springs in her shoes. Sometimes it wore me out to watch her. Where did she get so much energy? She was a freshman at college, working here over winter break. This resort was a popular retreat for college students—whether to play or work. I'd created a fictitious background that resembled everyone else's true story. I was a university student looking for work during winter break. When the students left, I'd probably move on as well.

Spike had hired me without asking for references. Maybe I had an honest face. Or maybe he'd been desperate for the help since students had arrived en masse to enjoy the slopes. Because he was dependent on seasonal employees, and most of the ones he hired didn't live in the town, he provided rooms in a couple of condos he owned. Lisa and I lived in the same one, our bedrooms across the hall from each other. It was the reason we'd become close. We saw a lot of each other.

"Wish me luck," she said with a wink. "I so want a winter romance, and he looks like the type to give a girl a good time."

Funny how she saw him as a good time, and I viewed

him as a journey straight back to hell. It was possible that he was here to enjoy the slopes, but judging by the way he was watching me, I had a feeling he was here to convince me to return to Wolford.

I handed the drinks to Romeo and Juliet. Three giggling girls who were eyeing Daniel as though he were their favorite flavor of chocolate shouldered their way to the front and breathlessly gave me their order: a white, a dark, and a milk hot chocolate.

As I turned back to the preparation counter, I glanced surreptitiously over to where Lisa was talking with Daniel. She was leaning on the counter as though she intended to take up residence there. Not that I could blame her. He had magnetic eyes and a wicked grin, the kind that made me want to join him in a smile. But I resisted the temptation. I didn't trust his appearance or the fact that I couldn't feel his emotions. Why was he blocking them? *How* was he blocking them?

Beyond the floor-to-ceiling plate-glass windows that provided an unobstructed view of the main street with its quaint shops and the towering snow-covered mountains in the background, the purple and blue shadows of twilight were descending. The crescent moon was already rising, yet still faint, giving it a ghostly, ominous appearance. A chill swept through me.

Wiggling her eyebrows, Lisa walked back toward me.

"He ordered a chunky chocolate. You know what that means. And I'm so tempted to put my theory to the test with that guy. Did you see his killer grin?"

Lisa had a theory that the more chocolatey a guy liked his hot chocolate, the better he kissed. If nothing else, she reasoned that he'd taste great. Daniel was the Big Bad Wolf, and she didn't even know it. His bottom lip was full and would provide such a nice cushion for mine. I wanted to kick myself for even wondering what his kisses might be like, because I suspected he was trouble.

"Apparently, though," Lisa continued, her brow furrowing, "what he really wants is you. He says you're friends, that you've been expecting him?" She ended her statement on a high note, questioning what he'd told her, wanting me to confirm or deny it.

Fear spiked inside me. He *was* here for me. The elders had probably sent him. I knew they wanted me to be at Wolford when I experienced my first full moon. And while legend said that I needed to go through my first transformation with a mate, I couldn't risk someone else's life if the harvester kept his promise and came for me. But I couldn't explain any of that to Lisa, so I simply lied. "Never seen him before in my life."

I carried the steaming mugs over to the three girls. As they paid, I said, "See that guy at the end of the counter?"

"He's a little hard to miss," White Chocolate said. "Even with that heavy jacket on, you can tell he's all muscle. And that face. He belongs on a Calvin Klein billboard."

"I wouldn't mind him keeping me warm all through the night," Milk Chocolate said with a giggle.

"Then this is your lucky day," I lied smoothly. "He's looking for someone to hook up with. And he has two friends who are just as hot."

"Really?"

"Where are they?" Dark Chocolate asked suspiciously.

"Parking their Hummer."

"They have a Hummer?"

"Oh yeah." I leaned in conspiratorially. "Their parents are mega rich. The guys just got in today and don't know anyone. They were flirting with me earlier, but, well, I have a boyfriend." I was becoming exceptionally skilled at lying. Before I'd run away from Wolford, I'd never lied, but I was astounded by how easily the false words rolled off my tongue lately.

The girls didn't even bother to wait for their change before traipsing around the corner to flirt with Daniel, so I dropped it into the tip jar. The money collected would be divided between all the employees at the end of our shift. It was never much, but my needs were simple: a good book, a warm fire, my own mug of hot chocolate, and hushed silence within myself. It was one of the reasons that I loved winter and had felt so at home at the resort. The snow absorbs so much sound and it creates a quiet that is more stillness than anything.

But with Daniel's arrival, my little haven was no longer comforting. I was going to have to leave. The sooner the better. With those three girls distracting him, now was my chance.

"Do you want to take him his order?" Lisa asked me.

"No, I'm going to the storeroom to get some more to-go cups." Before she could comment, I slipped through the swinging door that led into a hallway where the boss had his office. I felt a little guilty running out on Spike after he'd given me a chance—and he was so protective.

"You need any help, little girl, you let me know," he'd said. At six feet eight inches, everyone was little next to him, but at five foot four, I was especially so. And while I appreciated his offer for help, I knew I'd never take him up on it. He wouldn't stand a chance against a guy who could transform into a wolf at will.

I was grateful that his office door was closed as I slipped by. I didn't want to have to explain myself or possibly make the mistake of deciding he could help. As I snuck down the hall, I resented that I was being forced to flee before I was ready. I'd hoped to save up a little more money so I could travel farther away more easily. I didn't really have a final destination in mind. I'd thought

I'd have more time to prepare. I'd allowed my happiness and contentment to lure me into a false sense of security. *Stupid, Hayden.*

I hurried down the hallway, past the storage room. I grabbed my white parka from a hook near the back door. Slipping off my sneakers, I stuffed them into my backpack and pulled on my snow boots. I jammed on a red-and-white knitted cap and tucked my ponytail up beneath it. I tugged on my gloves.

I glanced back over my shoulder. I didn't want to leave the warmth and safety offered here. I desperately didn't want to leave the peace and quiet. But I knew I had no choice. I had to run. Fast. Now. No way was I going back to Wolford.

I shoved open the door and stepped out into the snow and cold. Before the door had even closed behind me, I was turning toward the woods where the shadows were lengthening and could hide—

"Going somewhere, Hayden?" a deep voice echoed around me.

My heart in my throat, I whipped around.

Daniel stood there, leaning against the wall, his arms crossed over his broad chest. He hadn't bothered with a cap. His black jeans outlined his long legs. His thick black jacket, still unzipped, added to his dangerous allure—as though the weather was no threat to him. His dark features and clothes made his green eyes all the more vibrant. Hot really wasn't the right word to describe him. Scalding, maybe?

Confidently he strode over to me, leaving a wake of footprints in the pristine snow. His eyes captured and held mine. I wanted to sprint toward the trees but knew he'd just follow at an easy lope.

He reached out to touch me, and I stiffened, preparing for the force of pride—I was certain he was swelling with it for locating me—to slam into me. Though I couldn't tap into his emotions with space between us, I knew nothing would prevent his feelings from reaching me when he touched me. Experiencing others' emotions was always more intense, more overwhelming when physical contact was involved. It was one of the reasons that I avoided it whenever possible.

I would have stepped back now, only I was curious. I wasn't accustomed to being around a Shifter and not knowing what he or she was feeling. But when Daniel's bare hand touched my cheek, all I felt was . . . warmth. Skin on skin. Roughened fingers gliding softly over my smooth cheek.

Even with this intimate contact, I couldn't feel what he was feeling. I didn't know what emotions were dancing through him. It made no sense. He was a Shifter. I should have experienced his passions long before he ever got this close to me. And when he touched me, I should have been rocked so hard that my own emotions would retreat.

But only my feelings were roiling through me. That stupid fear again, ratcheted up to panic now. But there was more. So much more. Anger, astonishment, disappointment, irritation, sadness. And fascination. Attraction. It was as though I'd just spun a wheel of fortune that was loaded with emotions instead of dollar amounts and they were rioting through me. Where would it stop? What would I feel when it was all done?

"Why bother running, Hayden?" Daniel asked quietly.

He leaned in close, so close, until I could no longer see his eyes, his cheek almost grazing over mine. I was too stunned by the sudden intimacy to move. I heard him inhale deeply, knew he was scenting me—a final, silent declaration to a job well done. I wondered why the knowledge made my knees grow weak. After our first transformation, all our senses heightened, but scent was always our most powerful.

"I'll just find you again," he said in a voice that was close to a purr.

He was making me feel crazy things. I didn't know what some of these stirring emotions were, what they signaled. The wheel of emotions finally stopped spinning, selecting one with which I was familiar.

Full-blown terror.

TWO

"I—I wasn't r-running," I stammered, then swore beneath
my breath because I never stammered. He'd unsettled me
and it made me angry that he had. The terror receded
and fury took hold, and I lashed out with a determined
tone. "Not that it's any of your business, but I was taking
a break."

"Uh-huh." With his green eyes twinkling, he reached
out and tapped the little red-and-white pom-pom on
my knit cap. I made an ineffectual slap at his hand that
served only to make him grin wider and made me feel
powerless. I was too familiar with that emotion. I'd never
liked it and disliked it even more now because it seemed

to amuse him so much. "You sure bundled up just to take a break."

I took a step back to get beyond his reach. "In case you haven't noticed, it's winter! Snow, sleet, ice, freezing temperatures. Never mind. I don't have time to give you a science lesson. I have to get back to work."

I started to trudge past him.

"You have to get back to Wolford."

His words stopped me dead in my tracks, and I spun around. I didn't want to plead or beg, and I fought to keep my voice even, but a bit of despair flowed into my words. "It's not safe for me there."

"And you think you're safe here? Alone?" He shook his head. "What were you thinking when you left Wolford?"

That my survival depended on it. "Are you not aware of the harvester's visit?" I asked.

"I was out on patrol that night. I didn't see it, but I saw the results."

It hadn't registered until now that he hadn't been one of the Dark Guardians in the clearing that night when Justin died.

"I heard it told you that you were next. We can protect you at Wolford."

I shook my head emphatically. "No, you can't. Safety there is an illusion. That's where the harvester will search for me. It won't know to look for me here."

I knew I was being reckless. Going through my first transformation alone brought with it the possibility of death. But I'd been studying the ancient texts, and I thought I might have found a loophole. I'd experienced what another Shifter had felt while transforming. All I had to do was mimic the emotion, follow the path he'd taken.

Daniel hesitated for a moment, and I felt a spark of hope that he might relent, but then he shattered it with his next words. "I'm sorry, Hayden, but the elders sent me to bring you back. It's my duty."

Not willing to give up easily, striving to buy myself some time, I folded my arms across my chest and jutted out my chin. "I know all about duty and responsibility. When I took this job, I gave my word that I would work here through winter break. This is the last weekend. You see how crowded it is in there. It's only going to get worse by tomorrow. I can't just leave. It's not fair to my employer; it's not fair to the other workers."

I knew that they probably could get by without me, but it was an excuse to buy me more time until I figured out my next move. I wasn't ready to go back to Wolford. And I certainly had no desire to be escorted back as though I'd done something wrong.

As though he understood exactly what I was thinking, he shrugged carelessly. "Through Saturday night, right? Most classes start back on Monday, so people will be heading away on Sunday. Why don't we talk about it when your shift ends?"

He sounded so irritatingly reasonable. I wanted him to leave and to leave me. I'd never flirted with a guy, had never tried to twist him around my little finger. But even if I had, Daniel didn't strike me as the easily manipulated type. "Okay, where do you want to meet?"

"I'll just wait for you inside."

"The shop doesn't close until nine. That's a long time to wait."

"It's all warm and cozy inside," he said. "I'll be okay for a few hours."

"Fine," I ground out.

I spun on my heel and stormed back into the building, annoyed that, with the snow, I couldn't actually tromp in order to make a statement. As I angrily removed my jacket and boots, I began mentally considering Plan B. And of course, thoughts of how best to evade Daniel made me think about him. My actions came to an abrupt halt.

Why didn't his emotions reach me? Was it because he had none? Was he a psychopath? Sociopath? Devoid of feelings?

I'd never met a Shifter whose emotions didn't come flying at me. I was a magnet for whatever they were feeling. So why not with Daniel?

The inability to access his emotions should have been

comforting, but instead it was scary. It wasn't natural. So what was wrong with him?

Or had a change happened within me? As my full moon approached, was I losing my empathic abilities? They'd seemed stronger than ever a couple of weeks ago. So why did they seem absent now?

It was all so weird. But I didn't really have time to ponder all the ramifications or possibilities. I had to get back to work. I stopped by the storage room and grabbed a plastic bag filled with paper cups and lids.

When I got back to the counter, Lisa gave me a confused stare. "Took you long enough. What'd you do? Get lost?"

I almost responded, *No, got found.* But I just said, "Took a quick break."

After arranging the cups on the shelf for easy access, I returned to my place at the counter. In the middle of the shop was a huge stone fireplace that was open on all four sides. Sitting areas had been arranged around it. I spotted Daniel lounging in a big stuffed chair, conveniently turned so I was once again in his line of sight.

"Hot guy was gone while you were," Lisa whispered. "Is there something you're not telling me?"

"Turns out I do know him."

"How could you forget a hottie like that? What's his name?"

"Daniel."

"Deets. I need deets."

I must have had a deer-caught-in-the-headlights look because she rolled her eyes. "Details. I need details. I swear that sometimes I think you were raised in a cave."

Almost.

"I'll explain everything later," I told her, knowing that I wouldn't.

I started taking orders, but the entire time, I felt Daniel's gaze on me. How could he sit so still, so patiently? And yet there was an undercurrent about him, as though he was amazingly alert, completely aware of everything going on around him, could strike within a heartbeat.

Shifters had an animal quality about them. When you can transform into a wolf, the attributes of a wolf are never far from you. You have that whole pack mentality. The alpha, the dominant, the submissive. It's a natural order for us. We mate for life. We hang around in groups. But sitting there, Daniel gave the impression of being a loner.

It made me want to connect with him, because I'd always felt like a loner among my own kind. Shifters weren't comfortable around someone who knew what they were feeling. It was only with humans that I felt as if I belonged—but even then I knew that I really didn't. They'd never accept a being who could shift. I had no place where I truly belonged. I straddled two worlds:

the one that brought me peace and the one marked with danger that was my destiny.

But Daniel belonged in the world of the Shifters. Did he just give the appearance of being a loner when he was around Statics? He didn't appear uncomfortable. He looked totally relaxed. Yet he was also alone.

I knew so little about him, and I couldn't deny that I was fascinated by him. But I recognized that my fascination was a dangerous thing.

"When he went after you, he left his hot chocolate at the counter and it got tossed," Lisa said, holding up a mug. "I made him a new one. Do you want to take it to him?"

Okay, her matchmaking attempts were starting to get a bit annoying. I knew she meant well, but how many ways could I say that I wasn't interested in Daniel? "No. If he wants it, he can come get it."

"You really don't like him. What'd he do?"

"He came here."

"Okay, that makes no sense. He's hot and he's nice. His coming here is an awesome thing."

"Take him the chocolate," I snapped—something I'd never done here in Athena. I'd experienced others' anger, had never been comfortable with it, so had worked really hard to keep myself as even-keeled around people as I could.

Lisa's eyes widened, but then she shrugged and went around the counter and over to Daniel. He smiled at her. She sat on the coffee table near him, and I wondered if he'd made her knees go weak. It irritated me that she could be swayed by his charm. The thought brought me up short. Was I feeling jealous because she was taking such an interest in him?

Actually, her interest in him could be a good thing. Maybe she could distract him. But as his gaze shifted back over to me, I realized he was not going to be easily sidetracked.

"Hey, can I get some service over here?"

I snapped my attention to a guy who was terribly sunburned. People were always underestimating what the sun could do in winter. They thought they could burn only if it was hot outside. "Sorry," I told him. "What'll you have?"

Darkness had fallen long before we started to close up. Spike came out of his office and flicked the lights to signal it was time for people to leave. He was a contradiction. With his shaved head and tattoos on his neck and arms, he just didn't look like the type of person who would make a living from hot beverages.

When everyone was gone except Daniel, Spike went over to him. "Sorry, bud, we're closing up."

"I'm waiting for Hayden," Daniel said.

Spike glanced back at me, and I knew that if I shook

my head, Spike would escort Daniel out. Or he'd try. I had a feeling that despite Spike's massive size, Daniel could whip his butt. So I nodded.

"Way to go, girlfriend," Lisa said, knocking her hip against mine.

I felt my cheeks grow warm with embarrassment, so I turned my attention to wiping down the counter. I was acutely aware of Daniel striding over.

"So tell me what I can do to get you out of here quicker," he said.

I had no desire to leave with him, but I also wasn't a huge fan of cleaning up. The lesser of two evils. I tossed him a damp rag. "Wipe down all the tables and put the chairs on top of them."

With Daniel's help, we finished with our closing procedures in record time. Sooner than I would have liked, I was bundled up and stepping out the back door with everyone else.

"Don't forget it's Thrilling Thursday. Catch you later at Out of Bounds," Lisa said with a wink and a grin before she led the others away.

"Thrilling Thursday?" Daniel asked with a dark eyebrow raised.

"Yeah, Lisa has a name for every night of the week. Manic Monday, Terrific Tuesday, Wicked Wednesday. You get the idea."

"Sorry I missed Wicked Wednesday."

It was difficult to stay annoyed with a guy who could flash a grin like Daniel could, but I resisted returning the smile, and even managed to narrow my eyes. "So how long have you been here?"

"Arrived this morning. Tell me about Out of Bounds."

"Not much to tell. It's a club. 'Out of bounds' is a ski term that refers to areas where it's illegal to ski. . . . Well, it's supposed to be a place for rebels."

"And you're a rebel?"

"I have my moments," I said, slightly insulted that he'd question me. After all, I'd run away, hadn't I?

"I noticed a burger place—conveniently named the Burger Place, by the way—at the end of the street," Daniel said as we walked around the building, back toward the main part of the village. "I could use some meat."

"I'm a vegetarian."

He jerked his head around, and his green gaze homed in on me as if he thought I was joking. Or suspected me of lying.

"I've eaten there before, though," I told him. "They have a grilled cheese sandwich, so we're good."

As we stepped onto the boardwalk that lined the street, he shoved his hands into the pockets of his jacket and said, "I've never heard of a Shifter being a vegetarian."

"Well, I'm not your ordinary Shifter."

"So I've been told."

I rolled my eyes, wondering exactly what the other Dark Guardians had said about me and my abilities. "I'd rather be normal."

I couldn't keep the wistfulness out of my voice. Maybe that was the reason that he didn't talk as we walked along the street. Or maybe he was trying to figure me out as much as I was trying to discern why a wall existed between his emotions and mine.

The elders were able to block their emotions from me, but they were the elders. They could do all sorts of stuff. They'd tried to teach me to block the emotions coming at me, but I'd had absolutely no success at it. I wondered if they'd given Daniel a crash course in holding back his emotions that he'd actually managed to master. Sometimes at school a teacher could explain a concept multiple times and I couldn't grasp what she was trying to teach, but the student sitting next to me could lean over and explain it—and it suddenly made perfect sense. I wondered if this might be the case here as well. Maybe he could explain blocking feelings in terms that I could more easily embrace. If Daniel could block his emotions, could I do it—but in reverse? He was keeping his emotions in. Could I do whatever he was doing to keep emotions out?

* * *

"So what do you know about me?" I asked.

We were sitting across from each other in a corner booth. I'd decided to go with a garden salad instead of a grilled cheese. He'd ordered a double-meat cheeseburger and onion rings. Hardening of the arteries wasn't a concern for us. When we shifted, our bodies naturally healed all ailments, including all the pitfalls of eating unhealthy foods.

"I know you have a gift," he said.

I stabbed a crouton. "It's not a gift."

Taking a bite from his burger, he studied me for a moment. He swallowed, then said, "Yeah, I can see how it wouldn't be."

I didn't want to like him, but his empathy was another new experience for me. He sounded as though he truly understood what burden I carried. Naturally no one at the boarding school knew that I was an empath because I couldn't tap into their emotions so it had seemed pointless to explain what I couldn't demonstrate for them. They were all Statics. I certainly wasn't explaining Shifters to them. That would have brought other complications. So at school I was blessedly normal.

"It's the reason I sought out a place where there were only Statics. Their emotions don't reach me. All I have to deal with is how I feel." He didn't say anything so I leaned forward. "Your emotions aren't reaching me either. How do you do it? How do you close them off? Did the elders teach you how to keep everything boxed in?"

"No, they didn't teach me anything, and as far as I know, I'm not doing anything to close off my emotions."

Incredulous, I stared at him. "But I don't get a sense of what's going through you. Your emotions don't touch me—*at all*. I've never been around a Shifter whose emotions don't touch me."

"So you don't know what I'm thinking?"

I shook my head. This was so difficult to explain. "I don't tap into people's thoughts. I can only sense the emotions: fear, anger, embarrassment, acceptance, lust—"

"Lust?" he interrupted me. "That must be awkward. So if some guy has the hots for some babe or she has the hots for—"

"I don't know who they're lusting after," I cut in. Thank God for that, but if they were in the throes of passion . . . it could be unbearable and such an invasion of privacy. "Because again, I don't know their thoughts. It's like a . . . how do I explain this? A ball of energy. No, a water balloon. It slams into me and drenches me, so I experience it as though it's part of me. All the physical reactions that a body has when we're afraid or anxious or in love . . . my body responds as though the emotion were mine. If several Shifters are in the area, then I can be hit with different emotions jumbling around inside me. Unless

39

someone is having a really intense emotional burst—then maybe the lesser emotions will be drowned out. If you couple that with my own emotions, it's incredibly over-whelming and confusing. But I don't feel that when I'm someplace that's inhabited with only full humans."

He either didn't know how to respond to my lengthy discourse on what it was to be me or he was thinking about it, trying to make sense of it. I studied him for a minute. His story was that he'd come to us from another group of Shifters, but I didn't know if anyone had checked it out. I thought about how easily I'd convinced Spike and the others that I was a college student on winter break—just looking for a temporary job. Perhaps Daniel wasn't a Shifter after all. Like Brittany. Her father was human, her mother a Shifter, so I supposed she was part Shifter, but her human side dominated. She didn't have the ability to shift, and her emotions never touched me. Was Daniel a mixture of Shifter and human? Or was he maybe a full human who had lied to infiltrate our clan? But then the question would be why? And he had managed to find me so he had mean tracking skills. I couldn't help but be impressed.

Last summer, when I'd been at Wolford for a couple of weeks, I'd overheard other girls talking and giggling as they whispered about guys, comparing their wolfish attributes, but I'd never understood their interest. Until now. For the first time in my life, I was curious about another Shifter's fur.

Our individual wolf coats are one of a kind, although it usually matches our hair to some extent. Like my sandy blond hair meant that I would be a light-colored wolf. Daniel with his black hair would have black fur. But there are still differences. Would it have a bluish tint? Would it be like a black hole? Like a night sky?

But I couldn't recall hearing anyone talk about what he looked like in wolf form. And I hadn't seen him that night in the clearing. How convenient. And if I thought about it too much: suspicious. I furrowed my brow. "But I get nothing coming from you. And I don't recall anyone ever describing you in wolf form. Are you a Static?"

He laughed, a deep rich sound. "No. Don't you think the elders, the other Shifters, would sense if I was?"

He had a point. Shifters could sense other Shifters, but only after our initial transformation. Everything changed when we were touched by our designated full moon. I didn't want to contemplate all that awaited me—even the possibility of death.

"Yeah, I guess," I muttered, wanting an easy explanation. "But if you're a Shifter, why are your emotions cut off?"

"I don't think they are." He dipped an onion ring into the ketchup and proceeded to eat it as if I wasn't dealing with an incomprehensible situation here. How could he be so unaffected? It irritated me that he wasn't willing to help me solve this puzzle.

"Why aren't they slamming into me?" I persisted.

"I don't know."

"Are you doing something to hold them back?"

"If I am, it's subconscious. Or maybe it's because we're not at Wolford. Have you ever sensed Shifters' emotions when you weren't at Wolford?"

"Yes." I'd lived with my parents in Tarrant, before they'd died. Humans and Shifters resided there, although the humans weren't aware of our abilities. The small town was near the national forest that we considered our true home. As a child, I'd felt Shifters' emotions—even when we were on vacation. My parents tried to take me places where there would be mostly humans, but Shifter families enjoy Disney World as much as humans do. I'd gotten lucky with Athena.

Daniel distracted me from my thoughts when he set his elbow on the table and bent his arm until his fingers touched strands of my hair. I'd released my hair from its clip before leaving work. Now it hung loose past my shoulders. "So you don't *know* what I'm feeling right now?" he asked.

Swallowing hard, I thought it would be extremely easy to lose myself in his eyes, especially when he acted as though touching me was the most natural thing in the world for him. Why was he so comfortable around me when I was so uncomfortable around him? I'd never before flirted with a guy. I'd watched Lisa, picked up a few tips, but I'd never tried them out. As much as I wanted to with Daniel, I knew that he was here on a mission to take me back to Wolford. I didn't want to fall under his spell. I turned my gaze away from him. "I think you're messing with me."

He kept his hand where it was, his fingers touching nothing but air now, his gaze roaming slowly over my face. "It must be very hard to be you."

"You are the king of understatement."

Slowly he sat back. "I know what you're feeling toward me. Anger. Resentment. You're no good at hiding it. But I'm just the messenger, Hayden."

"No, you're not. You're the bounty hunter." I leaned forward again, wanting him to see the desperation in my brown eyes. "Why don't you just go back and tell them that you couldn't find me?"

"Because three days ago you turned seventeen. Happy birthday, by the way. And in nine days your full moon will roll through the sky and you'll go through your first transformation. You know a female Shifter risks death if she tries to go through it without a mate. And then there's the harvester. You can't face it alone."

"I *have* to face it alone," I insisted. "The harvester snatches a soul at the moment of transformation. To guide me through it, a mate would transform at the exact moment that I do—and *bam*!" I slapped my palm on the table for emphasis, not that my action startled him. His eyes didn't so much as widen in surprise. "The harvester has us both."

He assumed that stillness I'd seen in him earlier. There was only one movement: a slow blink.

"Do you see now?" I asked. "Do you understand?"

"The elders insist that I bring you back. Explain to them what you think will happen."

"It would be better if I just stay here where there are only Statics. There's a chance the harvester won't even find me here. I've studied the transformation process as it's described in the ancient texts. I really believe I can survive the physical pain."

"Hayden." He took my hand. Again I was surprised by the warmth of his touch and the spark of physical sensation it sent through me. But not one iota of emotion accompanied it. "Even if I don't take you back to Wolford, your mate won't let you go through your first transformation alone."

Rolling my eyes, I scoffed. "Look, this is all moot. I don't even have a mate."

"Yes, you do. The elders chose one for you."

God! They were worse than old maid aunts butting their noses into everything. Why couldn't they just leave well enough alone? "They had no right—"

"They had every right. They're not going to condemn a girl to death. They've chosen mates before for others when a guy doesn't step forward."

In frustration I shook my head. "I won't accept him. Why would I put him at risk of facing the harvester and possibly dying without his soul secure? Why would they? They can't control everything. They have to let this go."

I was agitated, upset. We sat there in silence for a minute, while his thumb stroked over my knuckles. Back and forth. Almost hypnotic. I felt my tension easing away, found myself falling under his spell. I realized with alarm that he could probably convince me to return to Wolford with him without his actually uttering a word. With his calmness, his belief in his mission, his ease with intimacy, he was incredibly persuasive. It was unsettling when I stopped to think about it, because in truth we were practically strangers. We'd never even talked at Wolford, and he'd certainly never expressed an interest in me.

Then curiosity got the better of me. "So who'd they choose . . . to be my mate?"

He released my hand and touched my cheek, his eyes never straying from mine.

"Me."

THREE

"Are you totally insane?" I asked, forcing myself not to shriek and draw attention to us. "You agreed to their crazy idea? Did you not get notified that I'm on the harvester's playlist?"

He just looked at me as though he found me amusing.

I didn't understand how a guy could let men who were old enough to be his grandfathers choose his mate. They'd tried to match him up with Brittany last summer, but she'd ditched him for Connor.

Okay, ditched was too harsh. Brittany had been in love with Connor forever, but he'd declared Lindsey as his mate, but then Lindsey fell in love with Rafe. . . .

Suffice it to say that we had our own daytime soap going on back at Wolford.

Since Daniel was once again on the prowl for a mate, I guessed the elders had decided I would work well. I didn't understand why someone hadn't latched on to him before. If I were a normal Shifter, I certainly wouldn't complain that they'd chosen him for me.

But I wasn't normal. And I had a monster after me. I couldn't do that to him—put him at risk like that. Why would he ever think I would?

As though reading my thoughts, he said, "The elders are scouring through the ancient texts. They're going to find a way to defeat this thing. But you need to be at Wolford for their knowledge to do you any good. It's safer there."

"You don't know that. They don't know that. Why? Why would you want to be my mate? During the bonding all your defenses would be down. You'd be as vulnerable as I am. Why would you do that?" I knew I was repeating myself, but I didn't know how else to make my point.

"I like to live dangerously," he said.

"Yeah, well, then, take up bungee jumping."

I got up out of the booth and headed for the door, acutely aware of his following me. My flight response warned me to head to the condo and prepare for my escape.

But this could be my last chance to mingle with a crowd and not be blasted with everyone's emotions. So while I knew it wasn't a wise move, when we stepped outside of the Burger Place, I said, "I'll catch you later," and turned away from the direction of the condo where I lived. Besides, I hoped by being casual that I'd throw Daniel off so he wouldn't be suspicious. I needed him to be less vigilant if I was going to make a break for it before the night was over. People were strolling along the boardwalk, some heading home, some going in the direction I was.

"I'll walk you home," Daniel said, falling into step beside me.

"I'm not going home."

"You will eventually."

I spun around. He wasn't even startled by my move, as though he'd expected it. That irritated me. "Look, I get it. You're here to take me back to Wolford. You gave me a reprieve until Sunday, so until then I'm going to carry on with a normal life." Or what was almost normal for me.

"I won't interfere."

"You will. Your very presence interferes."

"I'm not leaving you alone, Hayden. Just in case you decide to take another"—he smirked—"*break*."

"What does it matter since you can find me anywhere?"

As three guys brushed past us, we both stepped closer to the building. Somehow I ended up with my back to the wall, and Daniel rested his forearm above my head. "Don't be a pain in my butt," he said quietly. "I compromised. Gave you a few more days here. Now you compromise and accept that those days and nights are going to include me."

My heart sped up at the thought of him spending all night with me. Honestly I'd never been this close to a guy—where I could actually smell his scent. One disadvantage to attending an all-girls school. Daniel smelled of the outdoors, a woodsy fire, sharp pine. I swallowed. "Not the entire night."

"That's your call. But until you're safely tucked in, I'm at your side."

Images of him in bed with me slid through my mind. What was wrong with me? I was feeling way out of my element. I shoved him out of the way, which was surprisingly easier than I'd expected, but I suspected it was only because he was willing to move. "Okay, fine. I'm going to Out of Bounds."

"I figured."

"You're irritating, you know that?" I asked as I began striding down the boardwalk.

"You only think that because we're at cross-purposes."

"Oh, and just so we're clear? The elders may have chosen you to be my mate, but until I accept you, you're not. Based upon what I've seen of your pushy attitude so far, I wouldn't get that tattoo just yet."

Tradition had it that a male Shifter would declare or claim his mate and then have a symbol representing her name tattooed on the back of his shoulder.

Daniel laughed. It was a rich, pleasing sound. "The elders don't know you as well as they thought," he said. "They told me you were biddable."

"Biddable?" Accustomed to the elders and their quaint words, I had a crazy urge to laugh. I couldn't take offense. They *didn't* know me. "Does anyone use that word anymore?"

"If you ask me, the elders always talk like they're living in another century."

"Because they are, buried in the ancient texts, concentrating on the past. They leave it to the Dark Guardians to determine the future."

"It's a strange combination. And talk about strange combinations . . ."

We'd arrived at Out of Bounds. The rustic building was the last place you'd expect to hear rock music blasting out of.

"That noise doesn't bother you?" Daniel asked.

"I can deal with the external stimuli. It's the internal

50

that overwhelm me. But if you don't like the music—"

"You're not going to get rid of me that easily." He flashed that grin that had mesmerized Lisa and he opened the door.

Inside, people were lined up three deep at the bar. Almost every table was occupied. Some couples were dancing in front of the band. I saw Lisa standing on a chair, waving at us.

"Over there," I said, and wended my way between the tables and people.

When we arrived, we took off our jackets and draped them over the backs of chairs while Lisa made quick introductions. The guy with her was Eric. I'd never seen him before, but she clung to him as if they'd gone steady for years.

"Eric got us a pitcher of beer, but we have to share the mug," Lisa explained.

"We're underage," I reminded her.

"Hence the reason we have to share the mug." She leaned forward. "So, Daniel, tell me about yourself."

"Not much to tell." He turned to me. "One mug at a table of four is bound to get us all carded. I'm going to get a soda to throw off suspicion. What do you want?"

"The same."

As he stood, he leaned in and whispered, "Don't go anywhere."

He disappeared, and Lisa grabbed my arm. "Okay, there is definite chemistry between you two. Is—"

"What kind of chemistry?" I interrupted to ask.

"Sparks. Sexual. You know. So is he an old boyfriend or what?"

"What."

She began to shout louder. "Is he an old—" I stopped her with a laugh. "No, he's a *what*. Not an old boyfriend. Just someone from back home."

"Which is where exactly? Spike thinks you're in the witness protection program or something because you don't tell us anything about yourself. You're all Miss Mysterious."

"I just want to be anonymous."

"In other words, mind my own business."

"If you don't mind."

She laughed. "You are too polite."

Then, thankfully, she turned her attention back to Eric. And two seconds later I wished she hadn't, because they were lost in a steamy lip-lock. I slipped away from the table and went into the game room, where pool tables were set up. Most of the tables were occupied so I stood against the wall pretending to watch the players. Across the room was a hallway that led to the restrooms. I'd been here before, so I knew that at the end of it was a door that led outside. I was considering my odds of a successful escape when a mug of soda appeared in my line of vision.

"Nice try," Daniel said.

"If I was planning to run away, I wouldn't be standing here. I'd be gone already."

"How did you do it anyway?" he asked. "Escape Wolford."

Shrugging, I sipped my soda. "It helped that a snowstorm hit later that night to cover my tracks. And everyone was preoccupied with what had happened to Justin." I tried not to think about it, but I couldn't help saying, "It was awful."

"I can't even begin to imagine. They said you felt—"

"Yeah," I interrupted.

"I'm sorry you had to go through that. I'm sorry that Justin did, too. I liked him. We all took what happened to him hard. Most of us had convinced ourselves that the story of a harvester was just a fairy tale."

"I could feel the souls. . . ." I shook my head. "I don't want to talk about this, not here, not now."

He nodded as though he totally understood. Then he asked, "So you play pool?"

"Lisa taught me."

"Let's play a game, then."

It was a distraction, and right then, I needed a distraction—badly.

"What are we going to play for?" I asked as I followed him over to the pool stick rack.

"What do you want to play for?"

"If I win, you leave without me."

He was reaching for a pool stick when my words hit him. Stopping, he studied me. "Are you that good?"

"Maybe."

He shrugged. "Okay. If I win, you have to accept me as your mate."

"That's ridiculous. You don't select your mate based on the outcome of a game."

"But you're willing to risk your life on it. You don't seem to get it, Hayden. You're in danger here. I'm the best chance you have of surviving what's coming."

His tone wasn't cocky or boastful. He really believed it. Unfortunately I believed his best chance of surviving to live to an old age meant me going my own way. Reaching for a stick, I skimmed my hand over the wooden rack. I felt a sharp pain. "Ouch!"

"What is it?" Daniel asked, grabbing my hand.

I tried to pull free, but he had a strong grip.

"Just a splinter, I think. Let me see," I ordered.

"I see it."

I jerked. He yanked.

"Hold still," he demanded.

"I can take care of it."

This time, he lifted his head and pinned me with his gaze. "Hold. Still. Please?"

At that moment I realized he never backed down. I also suspected he never lost. He was like an immovable force. A couple of people were looking at us. I did not want a scene. I swallowed hard and nodded.

He turned his attention back to the stupid splinter. He had large hands, long, slender fingers. I was surprised he was able to grip the splinter and pull it free. A tiny bit of blood pooled on my palm. I watched in amazement as he lifted my hand and sniffed. Then he rolled out his tongue and licked away the blood.

Heat speared me clear down to the soles of my feet, and my toes curled so tightly that I wasn't sure they'd ever straighten back out.

"Blood scent," he said, his voice a deep growl, his gaze back on mine, causing me to grow so warm that I thought I might have to remove my sweater or boil. "The strongest. Now I'll always find you—no matter where you go."

I jerked my hand free. "What are you—a vampire?" My heart nearly seized up. "Is that it? Is that why I can't feel your emotions? Why you think you're immune to the harvester?"

"Don't be ridiculous. Vamps and Shifters don't mix."

"That's not an answer. It was a yes or no question."

He narrowed his eyes, sighed with impatience. "No. I'm not a vampire."

"What are you?"

He glanced to the side. The people who'd been watching had turned their attention back to their game. He slid his gaze back to me. "A Shifter."

"Not like any I've ever met."

"And how many have you met? Other than those at Wolford, I mean. There are different clans, different tribes. Maybe you can feel the emotions of only those who originated in Wolford."

I wrinkled my brow as I considered his words. "Why would where someone was from make a difference?"

"I don't know. Maybe it's something in the water."

"Okay, that doesn't make any sense. And I have been around Shifters who didn't come from Wolford." We were talking quietly so no one else in the room could hear us. "When I went on vacation with my parents, there were those I didn't know. And I still felt their emotions. It's just you. There's something different about you."

For the first time since he'd arrived, he seemed uncomfortable. His gaze darted briefly away from mine. "Let's change the stakes. How about if you lose you cook me breakfast in the morning?"

Why was he changing the subject? Was I on to

something? The room was becoming more crowded, and I knew any in-depth conversation was out of the question. But his reaction was something to ponder and consider. "And if I win?" I asked.

"I'll cook you breakfast."

"I have to be at work at six."

"Not a problem."

"Actually there is. No free tables."

He winked at me—I resented that so simple a gesture made my knees weaken—and grabbed a stick. I watched as he slowly surveyed the room, then he strode over to a table on the far side and just stood there. I could tell the two guys who were playing were growing increasingly uncomfortable, even though Daniel didn't do anything. He didn't threaten them, didn't speak to them. His nearness, his stillness, and his watchful gaze were enough. They left their game unfinished.

Impressed, I walked over and joined him while he began racking up the balls. "That was the same thing you did earlier in the day when you wanted that stool. How do you do that?" I asked.

"There are submissive Statics, just like there are wolves. You simply have to recognize them."

"And you're an alpha."

"All Dark Guardians are," he said quietly.

"That was really kinda mean."

He shrugged indifferently. "All they had to do was defend their territory by not leaving. I wasn't going to fight them for it." He stepped back. "You break."

I guess I couldn't really fault him for his approach to getting us a table. He hadn't been aggressive, but he gave off such powerful vibes—even standing still. He'd be the leader of the pack.

Although the Dark Guardians already had a leader: Lucas Wilde. But Daniel was right: All the Dark Guardians had alpha tendencies. They didn't back down from a fight. But they also recognized and respected the acknowledged leader. I'd always thought it took a lot of confidence in one's abilities not to feel threatened at taking orders. I had to admire Daniel for joining our group and blending in without creating any conflict. The elders had to trust his abilities to send him off on his own to find me.

I smacked the balls, watched them roll over the table, and since none dropped into holes, found myself glad that we'd changed the terms of the wager.

With an almost cocky grin, Daniel stepped up and bent over the table. I moved out of his way.

"Are you the only one the elders sent to find me?" I asked.

He looked over his shoulder. "Yes. Why?"

I shrugged. "They had a lot of faith in you."

"You weren't that hard to find once I caught your

scent." He smacked a ball, and it landed in the corner pocket.

"How did you know what I smelled like?"

He hesitated, hit a ball, and missed the side pocket. "I checked out your bed."

Okay, now I was blushing. I supposed I should have expected that answer. It would have been the place where my fragrance was the heaviest, where I'd tossed and turned and rolled all over the sheets. I wondered if Daniel had done the same—in wolf form—coating himself with my essence. Suddenly I was so warm that it was as if someone had built a fire right next to me. Shaking off the bed image, I moved into position—

"You ever beat Lisa?" he asked.

"Not so far. Why?"

"You're not holding the stick exactly right." Before I could respond, he moved behind me and put his arms around me, cradling me within the curve of his body. There was that intimacy again, him acting like we were already mates. I couldn't explain how comforting but unsettling I found it. How could I feel both at the same time?

"You're not my mate yet, you know," I said, my voice not entirely steady.

"Are you uncomfortable with the nearness?"

"I'm just not used to it. From guys, I mean. From

Shifters. The girls at school hugged and stuff. . . ." But it didn't make my legs feel weak, didn't make me wonder what his kiss might be like.

"So get used to it. I can't help you through your transformation if I'm not touching you."

And when he touched me, the harvester would touch him. It would be bliss and hell at the same time. As scared as I was whenever I thought about facing my first transformation, of maybe also facing the harvester, it scared me more to think of something happening to Daniel simply because he was trying to help me.

As he positioned my hands, his cheek was so close to mine that I could almost feel the bristles along his jaw.

"I heard that when Brittany needed a mate, the elders put the eligible guys' names in a hat."

Grinning, he nodded. "Yeah. Very low-tech dating service."

"Is that what they did with me? And you got unlucky again?"

"I volunteered," he said very quietly.

My heart stammered. "Why?"

"It was a challenge. I didn't have anything better to do."

So he hadn't been crushing on me from afar. Again I had conflicting emotions. This time they were relief and disappointment.

"You really know how to make a girl feel special," I said sarcastically. "I'm beginning to understand why Brittany didn't accept you as her mate."

"She didn't accept me because she loved Connor. I figured that out after ten minutes of talking with her. Is there someone else instead of me that you wish was here?"

"I don't even want you here."

"That's not an answer. It was a yes or no question." He was tossing back at me what I'd said to him earlier. "Is there?" he prodded.

The only person I could think of was my mom. "No," I reluctantly admitted.

"Then relax."

I gave him a questioning look.

"It'll make the shot easier to make," he said, with his now-familiar grin.

He released his hold on me and stepped back, but his eyes never wavered from mine, and I wondered at his true reason for volunteering. Maybe he needed to get away from Wolford as much as I did. Or maybe he just wanted to do something different. It couldn't possibly be that he was interested in me. How many times had we set eyes on each other before today? Half a dozen, maybe? None of this made sense.

I whacked the ball. It smacked into another ball,

sending it toward a pocket, then ricocheted off and hit another, forcing it down a side pocket. I missed the next shot, and Daniel proceeded to clear the table. I owed him breakfast.

"I pour a mean bowl of cereal," I conceded as we headed back to the room where the band was playing.

He laughed at that. I wished I could relax around him. But something wasn't right. I simply couldn't figure out what it was.

We joined Lisa and Eric, shared their beer until I was mellow. The music was too loud for us to do any talking, but I was aware of Daniel watching me, his gaze never straying, as though he suspected I had the ability to disappear in a puff of smoke.

Finally I said, "I'm ready to go."

We grabbed our jackets, said good night to Lisa and Eric, and went outside. Light snow had begun to fall. I knew the skiers would welcome it in the morning. I tried not to notice how comforting it was to have Daniel walking beside me. Even if the elders had designated him as the one to go through my full moon with me and we somehow managed to survive, I had no guarantee that the morning after he wouldn't lope away.

Going through the first shift was an intimate experience between mates. We couldn't shift with our clothes on, so it would be really uncomfortable and weird to go through it with someone you didn't love completely. The elders could order the Dark Guardians to do a lot of things—but no one could order a heart to love someone in particular.

And then there was the harvester to complicate things.

"So what was your first shift like?" I asked as we headed toward my condo.

Daniel shoved his hands into his pockets, and I sensed that he was hesitant to confide in me about it. I knew I was being nosey. Shifters didn't talk about their first time. It was a private moment—for the males especially because they went through it alone.

"Scary," he finally said.

"Is that why you didn't object to the idea of being my mate?"

He rolled his shoulders inward, then straightened. "Yeah. I figured if I could help you through it—why not? Besides, I've been at Wolford for six months now. I haven't connected with a girl. I'm an outsider. They trust me as little as you do."

It embarrassed me that he was able to read my feelings so easily. "Are you sure you're not empathic?" I asked.

"I'm sure." He got really quiet, and then he said in a low, emotion-laden voice, "It's painful, Hayden. The first time. Your body feels like it's tearing itself apart. I guess in a way it is. But after that, it's just amazing. There aren't words to describe it."

I heard the awe and wonder in his voice, which in a way made things worse. I knew without a mate that I risked death. There's a bond, a connection that develops and intensifies during the first transformation, but it has to at least be hinted at before that magical night.

I didn't want to go through this wondrous experience with a surrogate. But that's all Daniel was offering me. A one-night stand-in for the real thing. I couldn't even contemplate that it could develop into something more. Because I wasn't even going to accept the offer for a one-night stand.

When we got to the condo, he stayed at the bottom of the stairs while I climbed them to the porch. I put the key into the lock and opened the door.

"Good night, Hayden."

I looked back over my shoulder and forced myself to smile. "Don't forget to come by in the morning for that bowl of cereal."

His low laughter followed me into the condo. I hoped my parting words had assured him that I wouldn't try to escape. Because the truth was I had every intention of being gone before he arrived for breakfast.

FOUR

Plan B involved traveling light.

In my room at the condo I stuffed a couple of sweaters, a pair of jeans, and a few other essentials into my backpack.

It was long after midnight, and the condo had gone eerily quiet or maybe it just seemed creepy because of my clandestine preparation to depart. The silence reminded me of Daniel's stealthy arrival. I wondered how long he'd been observing me today before he made his presence known. It really irritated me that he could sneak around and I wouldn't know it. I'd always hated this burden I carried, and here I was complaining because the one time

I'd needed it, it had let me down.

I hadn't even asked Daniel where he was staying. Hotels and bed-and-breakfasts were located all through the town. Maybe he had a room somewhere. Or maybe he was simply going to shift into wolf form and curl up in the woods. The village was in a valley, surrounded by mountains and trees. He could find someplace to sleep. I wasn't going to feel guilty about any hardships he might suffer. I hadn't asked him to come searching for me.

After bundling up in my outside gear, I slung my backpack over my shoulder. I took one last look of longing around the room. I really had known happiness here. I was going to miss it.

Opening the door, I peered into the hallway. No one was around. Drawing on the hunting instincts of my kind, I crept toward the stairs. Cautiously I descended into the living room. No one had closed the drapes. Faint moonlight spilled into the room, enough to guide me.

I crossed the room and went out the back door, closing and locking it behind me as I stepped onto the deck. I darted down the wooden stairs and headed toward the shed where I'd parked the snowmobile I'd stolen at Wolford the night I'd made my escape. In anticipation of having to make another hasty retreat, I always kept the tank full. But when I got around to the shed and opened the door, I discovered the snowmobile was gone. I swore harshly beneath my breath. Of course. The elders must have given Daniel an extra key, and he wouldn't have trusted me not to try to make an escape using something that moved faster than my legs. He could have taken it at anytime after he arrived.

Fury lashed at me. I wanted to shriek, to tear into him. I stomped my foot in the snow, a less than satisfactory action because little sound accompanied it.

"Jerk," I muttered as I glanced around. I wouldn't have been surprised if he was hiding somewhere watching me now. "Double jerk."

I wished I could sense his nearness. Only I couldn't. What if he wasn't keeping watch? What if he thought taking the snowmobile was enough to deter me or that his charm was enough to hold me?

I was just stubborn enough to decide that if I started walking now, I could reach the next town by dawn. Who knew? Maybe they even had a bus depot.

I pulled a flashlight from the front pocket of my backpack, then adjusted the straps and weight on my shoulders. I trudged toward the trees. I was familiar enough with the area to know that the woods would provide me with some cover that the main road leading out of town wouldn't. Eventually I would connect with the winding road.

I was walking among the trees where the lights from town didn't penetrate when I finally switched on the flashlight. It was amazing how black the night could be when only a sliver of moon was in the sky. I had a terrific sense of direction, part of my natural wolfish instincts. I wasn't afraid of getting lost.

But the air was cold and I couldn't feel my nose. Several more hours of this wasn't the smartest thing I'd ever planned. And Daniel probably figured I was too smart to do something this stupid, so there was a chance that he wasn't watching me. The woods were filled with a thick silence. Somewhere a twig snapped—no doubt beneath the weight of snow and ice.

I'd always been comfortable in the woods, but suddenly a chill skittered down my spine. My breath hadn't been visible in the frigid dry air, but now it was. Just little wisps of fog. If it was at all possible, everything went even quieter. I couldn't explain it, but it was as though I'd suddenly been submerged in water. My ears had a strange ringing to them.

Then I saw the bluish gray mist rolling in slowly along the ground between the trees. I stopped dead in my tracks. It was a strange sight in the crispness of the snow-covered landscape. It crept silently, and yet it was almost like a living, breathing thing. Ominous. Creepy. It was only as high as my knees, but still I didn't want to walk through it.

It reminded me of the harvester's retreat. But it couldn't be here. It couldn't have found me.

The flashlight flickered and went dark. All I had now was a spark of moonlight. Yet the fog somehow seemed more visible.

Time to go.

I spun on my heel and slammed into something hard. Strong arms came around me.

Shrieking, I broke free, lashed out—

"Hey! Easy, easy!"

Recognizing Daniel's voice, I stopped flailing my arms and kicking. I sank against him, my breathing harsh. Taking the cold air so deeply into my lungs made my chest ache.

"Did you see it?" I asked.

"See what?"

I lifted my head to get a better look at him, but the darkness kept us both in shadows. "There." I turned around to point, and everything inside me stilled.

There was no fog, no mist. Only my flashlight, now working, resting on the ground where I'd dropped it, its light pointing toward the depths of the forest and revealing nothing beyond the snow and skeletal trees. A snow bunny hopped through the beam, and I nearly came out of my skin.

"You're afraid of a little bunny rabbit?" Daniel teased.

"I'm not afraid of anything. It's just that . . . there was something there."

Walking past me, he bent and snatched up my flashlight. "Like what?"

Okay, *fog* sounded even less dangerous than a rabbit. And since he wasn't there the night of the harvester attack, he hadn't seen what I and the others had. But still I confessed, "It looked like mist." Coming for me. Or at the very least, blocking my path. And now it was gone.

"'Looked like'? You think it was something else?"

I shouldn't have been surprised that he'd picked up on my wording. We came from a world where everything wasn't exactly as it appeared.

"I don't know. I mean, it was there and then it wasn't." I felt uncharacteristically paranoid.

He glanced around. I heard his deep intake of breath, knew he was scenting the air.

"I smell only the rabbit . . . and an owl. If that rabbit's not careful, it'll end up as a late-night snack." He handed me my flashlight. "So what are you doing out here? Taking a break from sleep?"

"Ha! Very funny," I said, turning on my heel and trudging back to the condo. "I was just out hiking."

His deep laughter rolled through me. "I'm beginning to think you're a compulsive liar."

"I work during the day. It's the only time I can enjoy the outdoors."

"Yeah, sure. Why can't you just accept that we're in this together?"

Because we're not. I didn't answer him. Instead I came to a stop, swung around, and studied the trees again. Everything seemed peaceful and quiet. Natural.

"You really were spooked," Daniel said.

"It was weird. It was like the night I saw the harvester."

His whole body language changed. He was suddenly very alert. "You think it's here?"

"I don't know. I don't know how it finds us. I just know that for a couple of minutes back there, it felt as though I wasn't alone."

"You weren't. I was following you."

I glared at him, before continuing back to the condo. "You could have alerted me to your presence sooner."

"Wanted to see what you were up to."

I came out of the forest near the shed. "You stole my snowmobile," I said tartly. "I should report you to the police."

"You're going to report *I* stole a snowmobile that *you* stole?" Daniel asked. "I don't think so."

"When did you do it?" I asked.

"Before I went in for hot chocolate."

"So you knew where I lived before we walked home." He didn't say anything. "Is there anything about me you don't know?"

"Sure. Your dreams. Who gave you your first kiss.

71

Your favorite movie. Mine is *Avatar*, by the way. Awesome special effects."

It was so difficult to stay irritated with him when he was so comfortable around me. But I was determined not to be distracted from my purpose by his charm. I marched over to the stairs. Guilt pricked my conscience. I stopped and studied him. "So where are you staying while you're here?"

He shrugged. "Around."

So I figured he'd probably been guarding me in wolf form and shifted back when he saw me going into the woods. In wolf form we had the ability to communicate telepathically with others in wolf form. I'd also heard that some true mates could read each other's thoughts while in human form. But to communicate with me now, Daniel had to be in human form.

I was still mad at him for taking my snowmobile, but he was just following orders. There was an old saying about keeping your friends close but your enemies closer. Daniel wasn't the enemy, but I was beginning to think that knowing exactly where he was would work in my favor. "You could sleep on the couch if you want."

He grinned. "Such a sweet invitation."

Okay, so I'd sounded a bit petulant. "Look, I'm mad about the snowmobile, but I'm trying to be nice."

"You don't have to try."

I rolled my eyes, and his grin widened as though he realized how corny his line sounded.

"Do you want the couch or not?" I asked. I knew his being on the couch meant I couldn't make another break for it tonight, but I probably couldn't anyway. It was late and I was tired, and Daniel was way too vigilant.

"Okay, sure," he said.

I glanced back toward the trees. Why did I have this creepy sense of being watched? And not by Daniel.

I hurried up the stairs and inserted the key into the lock. I opened the door and Daniel followed me inside.

"Nice," he said.

The living room was large with a fireplace and a flat-screen TV. A couch was nestled between two end tables in the sitting area in front of the fireplace.

"I'll get you some blankets," I said, and went to a hallway closet. I stretched up to grab the blankets and became intensely aware of Daniel reaching over me, his chest brushing against my back.

"I've got it," he said.

I slipped under his arm and watched as he grabbed the blankets and a pillow.

"I really appreciate this," he said. "I hadn't considered that all the hotels and bed-and-breakfasts would be full. Not that I mind sleeping in a tent, but a couch is better."

Dark Guardians spend their summers leading campers

through the national forest. They were into the outdoors in a big way. I knew Daniel had probably traveled on all fours, but once he got here, he would have purchased any supplies that he needed. It was easy enough to carry some cash in a collar.

"I guess you traveled on all fours," I said, wanting to confirm my suspicions.

"As much as possible, yeah. But we'll use the snow-mobile to get back to Wolford."

"So if you traveled in wolf form, where did you get the clothes?" I asked.

"Did a little breaking and entering when I got here this morning. Don't worry. I left money on the counter."

"I wasn't worried. Just curious. Make yourself at home."

He headed for the couch and I headed upstairs. Then I heard the front door open. I darted back down, just as Lisa was coming into the entryway.

"Hey," I whispered. "I'm letting Daniel use the couch."

"The couch?" she repeated as she joined me on the stairs. "He's definitely bed worthy. Looks like he knows his way around a good cuddle."

"We're not even friends," I muttered as we ascended the stairs. To change the subject I asked, "How were things with Eric?"

Shrugging, she stepped onto the landing. "He was okay, but we didn't hook up. Afraid seeing you with Daniel has me wanting more."

"What do you mean?"

We'd reached our bedrooms. She leaned against her doorjamb.

"There is obviously a real connection between you two. Like soul mates or something."

If that was true, wouldn't I feel it? And wouldn't that make it even harder to lose him to the harvester? "He's just a guy."

"You're either fooling me, or fooling yourself. I want to know what you have going on with the hot guy."

"I don't have anything."

"I think you do. You just don't know it yet. Good night," she said.

She slipped into her room and I went into mine. I got ready for bed. I lay there for a long time unable to sleep. Daniel wasn't just a guy. I wasn't convinced he was just a Shifter.

Then what was he?

FIVE

The next morning I woke up exhausted. Everything was unusually quiet, and when I checked my clock, I saw that I'd overslept. Everyone else was probably already at the shop.

I showered and dressed in jeans and a hunter-green sweater. Pulling my hair back, I studied my reflection in the mirror. My eyes were striking, caramel-shaded, just like the guy had mentioned yesterday. I wondered what Daniel thought of them, then chastised myself. What did I care what he thought?

Grabbing my jacket, I headed down the stairs and crept into the living room. He was still asleep, stretched out on the couch. Lying there, he looked like any normal teenage guy. He appeared completely human.

I wondered if in his dreams he saw himself in wolf form or human form. Did we dream when we slept in wolf form? As my time approached, the silliest questions were arising.

As quietly as possible, I made my way to the kitchen, took a bowl down from the cabinet, and poured bran flakes into it. I set it on the table and placed a banana beside it, along with a note: *Milk in the fridge. Enjoy your breakfast.*

I froze. What was I doing? Acting like we were a couple with little secrets and private jokes. I started to crumple up the note, then changed my mind. I didn't know what I was going to do about Daniel, returning to Wolford, dealing with the harvester, or my life in general. What I did know was that I was late for work.

I headed out the front door. As I started to go down the steps, a chill swept through me. It was different from what I'd felt when Daniel had watched me the day before. This felt menacing, ominous. I glanced around. I didn't see any—

Movement. I thought I saw movement in the trees. Something shimmered, something dark. Then it was gone.

"Don't get paranoid," I muttered.

When I got to the shop, I went in through the back door and hung my jacket and backpack on a peg. Then I went to the counter area, where everyone was busy setting up for the morning rush. Most of the orders would be to-go as people took their warm drinks with them and headed to the slopes.

"I can't believe you let him sleep *alone* on the couch," Lisa said as she reached past me for a packet of coffee.

"I told you. I barely know him."

"That's never stopped me." She wiggled her eyebrows at me.

I laughed lightly. "It's complicated."

"So un-complicate it."

Easier said than done. This was a conversation I really didn't want to have so I turned my attention to filling the hot-water urn.

"You're still in for Fantastic Friday, right?" she asked, obviously deciding to leave my love life for me to deal with.

I gave her a blank look.

"I've arranged for us to ride the ski lift to the top of the mountain at midnight."

Everything at the slopes closed down at dusk. But Lisa had connections. "Oh yeah. Sure. I'll be there."

"With hottie?"

Who knew what opportunities for escape might

await at the top of the mountain?

"Absolutely."

But I didn't have much opportunity to consider plans because Spike opened the front door and people crowded through it, anxious to get their hot beverages of choice. The morning was hectic as usual, and I had little time to wonder where Daniel might be. Although I was slightly disappointed not to see him among the sea of faces calling out orders. And that bothered me. That a part of me actually missed him, had been looking forward to seeing him. I didn't want to accept him as part of my life and all the dangers that involved.

Maybe he'd wake up with a change of heart and go back to Wolford without me.

Yeah, right, Hayden. As long as you're living in a fantasy world, you might as well believe that the full moon won't come either.

By midmorning the rush was over. Spike kept only one of us on duty during the day—until the late-afternoon rush hit. Today, thankfully, wasn't my day.

As I poured hot chocolate into my insulated mug, I considered trying to make another break for it, maybe convincing Spike to drive me to the next town, where I could catch a bus or something. Only I didn't even know if the next town had public transportation. I'd been willing to chance it last night, but now I realized that, with Daniel's determination, I needed a more concrete plan. Getting him off my trail wasn't going to be easy. I needed to borrow Lisa's laptop and research my options, maybe find a way to put him off my scent. Although considering how often he got close to me, my scent was probably ingrained now. I thought of him tasting my blood. I'd never known a wolf to care about blood scent. Daniel wasn't like any Shifter I'd ever been around, but then my exposure to them had been pretty limited.

As I trudged back to the condo, fresh powder began to fall. The thick flakes stuck to my eyelashes then melted. Wolford would be covered in snow as well. The national forest was near the Canadian border. Cross-country skiing was a popular sport in the forest. We had a few mountains, too, where Shifters might ski, but they had never been opened to the public for skiing. That didn't stop us from testing the powder or our own limits. It was the one time when I hadn't minded being around other Shifters because the emotions reflected the thrill of adventure.

During the height of winter the forest was closed completely to the public. It was so beautiful and peaceful out in the wilderness then. I'd spent some time exploring the woods when the emotions at Wolford had become overwhelming. It was a good thing that I enjoyed my own company, because often it was all I had. I'd relished the solitude. As much as I didn't want to go back to Wolford,

I couldn't deny that I missed it.

I went around to the back of the condo and stomped up the steps to the wooden deck. I dusted the snow off an Adirondack chair, sat down, pulled my knees to my chest, and sipped on my chocolate while enjoying what surely would be my last days of peace. I had a great view of the woods. Evergreens were sprinkled among the bare-branched trees. I watched as some deer walked through. And then, as though catching the scent of a predator, they bounded away.

I heard the sound of boots crunching on snow, getting louder as they came up the stairs. Even though I couldn't detect his emotions, I knew who it was, knew his gaze was homed in on me, because the hairs on my neck prickled, but it wasn't an entirely unpleasant sensation. It was more along the lines of anticipation—which irritated me. I didn't want him around. I brought my steaming chocolate to my face, allowing the mist to tickle my nose, anything to distract me from this strange reaction to his arrival. I didn't turn my head, just kept staring out through the wisp of steam.

I wondered when he'd left the condo, why our paths hadn't crossed, if he'd been out spying on me.

"Didn't trust me to come back?" I asked tartly.

"I'm not a fool, Hayden," Daniel said, his voice laced with humor, as he sat down in a chair beside mine.

It annoyed me that I amused him. "I didn't see you."

"I was there . . . watching."

"That's really kinda creepy, you know. They arrest people for stalking."

"I wouldn't have to do it if you'd give me your word that you wouldn't run off."

I glanced over at him. He was wearing a maroon sweater today, and I realized that he had some clothes stashed somewhere. "You'd believe me if I gave you my word?"

"Not on your life. Did you bring me one?" He indicated my insulated mug.

"No. Wasn't even sure you were still around."

He chuckled. "Right."

Then he took the cup from me and sipped on my chocolate. I wanted to lash out at him, but for some reason my vocal cords knotted up, maybe because my throat and chest had tightened. Watching him, the intimacy of our sharing a drink, was unsettling. He seemed so at home with me, totally relaxed, and yet there was still that alertness to him as his gaze wandered over the landscape in front of us. I could sense him listening intently, as if not quite believing the peacefulness surrounding us.

"Expecting trouble?" I asked as I reached over and regained possession of my cup. I almost turned it so I wouldn't touch where his lips had touched, but I could sense the dare in his gaze, so I sipped from the same spot he had.

"I always expect it. That's part of being a Dark Guardian."

I wrapped my gloved hands around my cup and felt the warmth seeping through. "I don't know how to make you understand how badly I don't want to go back," I told him.

"I don't know how to make you understand how imperative it is that you do." With a deep sigh he leaned forward, planting his elbows on his thighs and staring into the trees before us as though he had the ability to see clear through them. "Last night you asked me what I knew about you. What do you know about me?"

Not much, I realized.

"I know you came from Seattle."

"Not Seattle exactly but the area around there." He bowed his head, studied his clasped hands.

I eased up in my chair, trying to get a better read on Daniel and what he was going through. He was as still as a statue, as though he thought if he moved, he might crack or crumble. "Did something happen?" I asked quietly.

"My family—my parents, my older brother—were killed."

Empathy swamped me and brought tears to my eyes.

It was so strong, so powerful. I'd lost my own parents in a car accident. Shifters had this amazing ability to heal quickly—but only in wolf form. And when an eighteen-wheeler slams into you . . .

It was death on impact. No time to shift, no time to heal. The authorities said my parents wouldn't have even known what hit them.

I'd never willingly reached out to touch another Shifter. Even though I now knew that I wouldn't be slammed by Daniel's emotions, old habits are hard to break; long-held aversions are difficult to overcome. Still I forced myself to remove my glove. Taking a deep breath, I laid my trembling bare fingers over his hands. They were clasped so tightly that they felt like a solid rock. "I'm sorry. I lost my parents when I was a child. I know how difficult it is to lose your family."

He unclenched his hands, turned one over, and threaded his fingers through mine, studying the intertwining as if it was the most fascinating thing he'd ever seen. "Did you feel their emotions?"

My throat constricting, I nodded. "I shouldn't have. They were so far away. They'd left me at Wolford because they were going to celebrate their anniversary. Their tenth, I think. I don't know. I just know I was mad they'd decided to leave me. Then I felt them die. The elders said it was because of the blood connection that distance didn't matter. I woke up screaming. The fear was so intense but brief. Mercifully brief for me and for them."

He squeezed my fingers. "I'm sorry. I didn't mean to dredge up old memories."

"What happened with your family?"

He shook his head. "At the time I wasn't exactly sure. They were dead when I got there. We . . . our clan . . . it's not like yours. You're all a tight pack. We're more scattered. I thought if I came to Wolford I might find some answers."

"Did you?"

"The night Justin died. Like him, my family didn't shift back."

"Oh my God. You think it was a harvester?"

"I don't know for sure. Maybe. Like I said, they were dead when I got there. And they didn't shift back to human form."

"I'm sorry. I'm so sorry. Is that why you're so intent on taking me back to Wolford?"

"One of the reasons. Maybe I feel like I have amends to make. I couldn't do anything to help my family. Maybe I can help you." He brought my hand up, kissed my fingertips. Warmth sluiced through me.

"What are you doing?" My voice sounded like air leaking from a balloon.

He glanced over his shoulder at me and gave me a

crooked grin. "Changing the subject."

Irritated that he wasn't willing to share more, I worked my hand free of his and settled back in my chair. "So what are you going to do for the rest of the day?"

"Depends what you do."

"I plan to just sit here and enjoy the peace. Until about midafternoon, when I'll head to the shop to prepare for the late-afternoon/early-evening crowd."

"Sounds exciting. I'll probably join you for that."

Because he didn't trust me not to skip out on him. I was still planning to find a way.

"And what sort of description does Lisa give Friday night?" he asked. "Because I can think of a couple of words that start with *F*."

His eyes were twinkling. I thought if it weren't for the whole harvester situation and my approaching full moon, I might actually enjoy hanging around with Daniel.

"Fantastic Friday," I told him. "We're going to the slopes tonight."

"To do what?"

I shrugged. "Maybe ski. Sit on top of a mountain. Whatever. Lisa has connections."

"I'll definitely be joining you for that."

"Who said you were invited?"

He didn't respond with words. He simply gave me a feral smile, and I realized he'd never let me escape him.

But if I wanted to survive, I would have to find a way to.

When the hot chocolate was gone and the cold air had chilled our bones, we went inside. One of the channels was having a big bug marathon, so Daniel settled in front of the TV and watched as ants, then grasshoppers, then ants again terrorized the countryside. I curled up in a chair with a novel. Although mostly I found myself studying him instead of reading about uppity New York socialites at the end of the nineteenth century.

I couldn't deny that Daniel was sexy, strong, and seemingly unafraid of anything—including the havoc that a harvester might cause. I didn't want to be morbid, but my own life expectancy was likely to fall way below the national average. If I went through my first full moon alone, I could die. If I managed to survive, the harvester could be waiting for me—and I'd die. I increased my chances of surviving if I had a mate, but then he risked death if we weren't able to avoid the harvester.

Basically I was feeling screwed, confused, and wishing there was a simple answer.

I had a crazy idea: Why not spend what little time I might have left enjoying life to the fullest, preferably with a guy? And here I had one sitting on the couch, not more than five feet from me.

I was still bothered by the fact that I couldn't feel his emotions. It also bothered me that he had been out on patrol the night Justin died. I was taking Daniel's word that the elders had sent him. What if he was an emissary for the harvester?

My stomach dropped as though I'd just reached the apex of a roller coaster and was careening down at the speed of light. I didn't think I'd be safe at Wolford. But I wasn't certain I was safe here anymore either.

SIX

Later that afternoon a light snowstorm hit, and I blinked as the snowflakes landed on my lashes while Daniel walked with me to the Hot Brew Café. I prepared him a double-chocolate hot chocolate, which he took to the sitting area by the fireplace. Again he turned so he was watching me. I must have been growing accustomed to his presence, because it didn't irritate me.

Then the rush started, and I didn't have time to think about Daniel, full moons, or harvesters. It was a little weird that working hard was so relaxing, but it actually relieved some of my stress.

It must have shown on my face because when we

began closing up, Daniel walked over to me and said, "You actually enjoyed that."

"Yeah, I did." I liked being around people—human people. I wished I could experience the same sort of connection with my own kind.

When we were finished closing for the night, Spike let Lisa, Daniel, and me out the front door. A guy in a silver Range Rover was waiting for us. His name was Chip, and he was apparently Lisa's main squeeze for the night. He was husky and had a beard that made him look like an authentic mountain man. After introductions were made, Daniel and I climbed into the backseat and Lisa buckled up in the passenger seat.

"This is going to be so much fun," Lisa said. "Chip packed a picnic basket for us. We'll take it to the top of Devil's Grin."

"What's Devil's Grin?" Daniel asked.

"The tallest slope," Lisa explained. "Skiing down it is for the more experienced skiers. You can decide when we get there if you want to give it a try."

"So we can ski?" I asked.

"If we want. My friend Jake is a ski patroller. He's sorta throwing an unauthorized party on the slopes tonight. Lights will be lit but only on the lower slopes. His girlfriend, Trish, has access to the rental equipment. No charge for us."

"I can't believe how many people you know," I admitted, in awe that one person could have so many friends. Or how much they were willing to do for her.

"Oh, you know. I'm the party girl. Can't party alone."

But when we arrived, we discovered the party had been canceled. The ski patrollers were out in force, and they were far from relaxed. Some were pulling toboggans.

"Sorry, Lisa," Jake said. He was tall and slender. Like all the other patrollers, he wore a red jacket to identify himself. "Just before we closed the slopes, we learned that a nine-year-old boy got separated from his dad up on the mountain. We had the dogs out searching, but they've had no luck. We're pulling everyone in to regroup."

"That's awful," Lisa said. "What can we do?"

He gave her a tired grin. "Go home so I don't have to worry about you getting lost."

I exchanged a glance with Daniel, and while I couldn't read his mind or sense his emotions, I knew what he was thinking. But if the dogs hadn't had any luck, how could he?

I saw a flash of movement out of the corner of my eye and glanced back. A couple was sitting on a bench. The man had his arm around the woman, who was staring blankly at the snow and turning in her hands what looked to be a blue knitted cap.

"Are those his parents?" I asked.

"Yep," Jake said. "Mr. and Mrs. Smith, if you can believe it."

"Is she holding her son's hat?"

"Yeah, the dad found it near a tree. Unfortunately the storm that came through this afternoon erased any tracks."

I turned back to Jake. "Surely there's something we can do. We could make hot chocolate for the search patrols, if nothing else."

"That's a great idea!" Lisa exclaimed. "Let us do that."

"Okay, yeah, sure," Jake said. "They're actually filling thermoses at the first aid station. Just go introduce yourself. Trish is there. I've got to get back to the patrol." He glided away on his skis.

"You go on," I said to Lisa. "We'll join you in a minute."

She furrowed her brow, and I jerked my thumb over my shoulder and mouthed, *Restroom.*

Thankfully she didn't ask why I needed Daniel to stay with me if I was going to the restroom. I figured she was so upset by the boy's disappearance that she wasn't thinking clearly. She and Chip walked away.

"So you want to help fill thermoses?" Daniel asked.

"No, that was just a ploy so Lisa doesn't leave without us and we have an excuse to hang around. Do you think you can find the boy?"

"I don't know. The dogs couldn't, but I'm willing to give it a try. I'll need you to stay close, though. Carry my clothes so I'm not stranded without them."

I nodded. "Okay."

"Let's talk to the parents, then."

We walked over to them. They barely noticed our arrival, their worry was so intense. Daniel crouched in front of the mother and I knew it was because he wanted to get closer to the cap, to smell the scent of the boy. Wolves, like dogs, have incredible olfactory senses. They can pick out individual scents. It was the reason they were so good at tracking.

"We're sorry for what happened to your son," Daniel said quietly.

The mother, with tears in her eyes, just nodded.

"What's his name?" I asked.

"Timmy," the dad said.

"Tim," the mom corrected with a wavering smile. "He decided he was getting too big for Timmy."

"Thought he was big enough to go off on his own," the father added.

"Which slope were you on?" I asked. I could have asked Jake, but I was trying to provide Daniel with the

93

time he needed to hone in on the scent he wanted.

"Misty Trail."

"I'm sure they'll find him," Daniel said.

Again the parents just nodded. I felt so helpless as we walked away, but I was grateful that I couldn't feel what they were feeling. We stopped by a map of the area that had all the slopes marked. "There it is," I said, touching a trail far to the north.

"We're going to need to get you a flashlight, so you can follow my paw prints," Daniel said.

"I actually have a penlight in my pocket." He looked at me, and I shrugged. "Never know when it'll come in handy."

Daniel, though, with his keen senses would be able to see in the dark. I didn't want Lisa to worry about us, so we went to the first aid station. I told her that Daniel had search and rescue experience and we were going to join in the search. One of the workers showed us on the map exactly where the father had last seen his son. I grabbed a hot thermos, and we headed out before anyone realized we weren't sanctioned to be searching for Timmy.

We started up the mountain. I didn't have any worries about getting lost. I knew Daniel would find me, and I knew he would be able to lead us to safety. Strange how this afternoon I'd contemplated for a brief time that maybe he couldn't be trusted and now I was putting my life in his hands.

We hit the ski lift that would take us to the top of Misty Trail. It was still running so the patrollers could use it. We took up our position and dropped onto the bench when it hit the backs of our legs. I wasn't sure how it happened, but Daniel's arm ended up around my shoulders. I wondered if all guys were as into touching as he was. I'd gone so much of my life without the touch of Shifters that in some ways I was starving for the intimacy. And Daniel seemed to be so good at providing it.

"Do you ski?" he asked as we swung out and up over the slope. There was a little more moon tonight. It was almost to its first quarter. A little more moonlight glittered off the snow. It was stunning. I wanted to be out here sometime when I had no worries.

"Yeah. You?"

"Some." He lifted the hand that had been resting on my shoulder and stroked my cheek. "I think tonight could have been fun."

A shimmer went through me as I realized he was focused on my lips, which suddenly parted of their own accord. I'd read about smoldering gazes, but wow, his was enough to warm me from my head to my toes.

"Get ready," he said.

"For what?" I wasn't sure that I wanted to be warned that he was going to kiss me. I just wanted him to do it.

95

"To stand."

"Wha—"

Then my feet were touching the ground. If Daniel hadn't practically lifted me off that bench with his one arm around me, I would have either face-splatted or continued back down the slope as the bench swung around to begin its journey downward. He then moved me out of the way of the next swing.

"This way," he said, taking my gloved hand in his and leading me down the incline.

It took me a moment to come out of the haze, to get my bearings, and to remember we were searching for a lost boy. Part of me wondered if Daniel was manipulating me to make sure I didn't run off or if he was finding himself as intrigued with me as I was with him.

How had this happened in only one day? Yesterday we'd been virtual strangers, and now I was yearning to know the flavor of his kiss. It was like he was doing whatever he could to make me want to be his mate. But was it out of obligation to the elders or desire for me?

We walked several minutes before we reached the slope we were searching for.

"Okay," Daniel said, releasing my hand. "I'm going behind that brush over there. Give me five minutes, then come get my clothes, and follow my trail."

"Five minutes?"

"Hey, until you accept me as your mate, I'm not taking any chances that you'll see my bare butt."

In spite of the circumstances I smiled. We stared at each other for several moments, and I wondered if he was going to finish what he'd seemed to want on the ski lift.

He turned away, then twisted back around and cradled my chin, holding me steady, his eyes looking deeply into mine. He leaned in. "Warning. If you use this opportunity to run, I *will* find you."

Before I could respond, he was loping to the bushes, his long legs eating up the distance. "It never occurred to me," I finally called out.

Although it had. With him concentrating on finding Tim, I could be long gone before he realized I wasn't following him. But how would I ever look at myself in the mirror if I took advantage of a tragic moment like this?

I heard the rustling in the bushes, knew he was removing his clothes. When things got silent, I waited for several minutes. Then I turned on my flashlight, walked to the bushes, and gathered up his garments. I stuffed them beneath my jacket to keep them warm and to give myself a little more insulation. Then I dropped his coat over my shoulders.

I started following his trail. The snow was deep, and he was moving fast, so the paw prints weren't distinct, but I could see the path he was taking clearly enough. I searched up ahead, trying to catch sight of him, wanting to know what he looked like in wolf form. Before yesterday I'd had little interest in him. Now I wanted to know every detail.

The going was rough in spots. The wind howled down from the mountains. Occasionally I'd take a small sip of hot chocolate, just to circulate a little warmth. But I wanted to leave the majority of it for Tim.

I'd been walking at a brisk pace for almost an hour when I heard, "Hayden."

I spun around, wielding the flashlight until its beam fell on Daniel standing behind some brush. "Did you find him?"

"Yeah. Toss me my clothes."

I did, and although I couldn't see anything, I turned my back to give him a little more privacy. Didn't want him thinking I'd accepted him as my mate. "Is he okay?"

"He's in a little enclave, not too far from here. He was out of it at first, really cold, but I built a small fire, then curled around him until he started to stir."

I knew after he'd prepared the fire that he'd returned to wolf form to comfort Tim. Daniel's fur and the warmth of his wolf body would have been heavenly to the little boy. He would have left when Tim started to wake up.

Daniel came out from behind the bushes and grabbed my hand. "Won't take us long to get back to him."

Fewer than ten minutes later I saw the boy sitting in the small natural shelter, his arms wrapped around his drawn-up knees, his eyes wide.

"Hey, buddy," Daniel said as he draped his coat over the boy. "Ready to go home?"

Tim nodded his head briskly. I'd never served as a forest guide, but a lot of the Dark Guardians did. Their covert job was to keep campers away from Wolford, but often they had to go in search of lost campers. Watching Daniel with Tim gave me a warm, fuzzy feeling, and I wondered how many campers he may have helped.

While I gave Tim his fill of warm hot chocolate, Daniel made sure that the fire was completely out. Then he boosted Tim onto his back. Tim was wearing Daniel's jacket over his own ski jacket.

"You're going to get cold," I told Daniel.

"Nah, we'll move fast."

And we did. I wished we'd thought to borrow someone's radio. As it was, no one knew we'd found Tim until we got to the ski lift. Some of the members of the ski patrol were standing around talking, trying to determine their next move when they spotted us. A shout went up. I heard the crackle of a radio as someone called down to the first aid station.

Jake took Tim from Daniel, handed Daniel his coat, and moved to a better-lit area so they could check Tim over before taking him down the slope on a sled.

"They'll take care of him now," Daniel said as he guided me toward the ski lift, and I realized he was anxious to leave before we drew too much attention to ourselves. They'd no doubt start asking questions that we didn't really want to answer.

As soon as my butt landed on the ski lift bench, exhaustion claimed me. Maybe it was the adrenaline rush of searching for and finding Tim finally waning. Or the effort of hiking through the snow, trying not to get too far behind Daniel.

Somehow his arm was once again around me. This time I gave in to it and leaned into him, placing my head in the nook of his shoulder.

"You were awesome," I said.

"Couldn't have done it without you. You were great at keeping up."

"I wanted to see you in wolf form," I said wearily.

"You've seen one wolf, you've seen them all."

"Not true. Each wolf looks different. Are you solid black?"

"Yes. Well, except for my eyes."

"I'll bet you're beautiful."

He didn't say anything to that. Maybe he understood that exhaustion was making me say things I wouldn't say under normal circumstances. I was so lethargic that I almost felt a little drunk.

He skimmed his thumb along my chin. I tilted my face to look up at him and discovered that his mouth was incredibly close to mine.

"I promised myself if I found him, I'd take a reward," he said softly.

I furrowed my brow. "His parents were offering a reward?"

"No. But I've been denying myself something I wanted."

His lips brushed across mine, so soft, so gentle. I could feel him holding back. I wasn't certain I wanted him to, but I also knew that I shouldn't encourage him, that I shouldn't lead him to believe I'd accept him as my mate.

I was still facing uncertainty and danger when the next full moon would roll around. I didn't want him sharing in it, risking his life for mine.

He drew away, a possessiveness in his expression that thrilled and terrified me. I wasn't going to get rid of him easily.

The problem was I was no longer certain I wanted to.

I lay in bed, staring at the moonlight filtering in through the window. How could something that looked so lovely and harmless be fraught with such dangers?

We'd joined Lisa and Chip at the first aid station. Lisa had been amazed that Daniel had found Tim. Daniel had modestly told her that it was nothing, that he'd done a lot of tracking in the woods. Which he probably had.

We'd returned to the condo and had our picnic on the floor in the living room. Wasn't quite as romantic, but I wasn't the only one who was tired and cold. Shortly afterward, Chip had left, Daniel had stretched out on the couch, and Lisa and I had gone to bed.

Only I couldn't sleep. One more day. One more night. And we'd be leaving.

I wasn't convinced going back to Wolford was the best move.

I got out of bed, threw on some sweats, and crept down the stairs into the living room. Daniel was staring at the ceiling, his hands shoved behind his head. His gaze came to rest on me. I padded over and sat on the coffee table.

"I'm afraid if I go to Wolford that I'm going to put others in danger. I'm afraid if I have a mate that the harvester will snatch its soul when we shift. I'm not sure Wolford is safe. I just . . . I don't know. If I accepted you as my mate, we could stay here. I could face my full moon here."

Slowly, so very slowly, he sat up, twisted around, and faced me. "Do you trust me?"

Did I? He was the type of person who cared enough to rescue a little boy. I nodded.

He took my hands. "If the harvester comes here, I can't save either of us. At Wolford we stand a fighting chance of defeating it, of surviving. The Dark Guardians are there. The elders. We know what we're up against now. They didn't know with Justin."

What he said made sense. If the harvester found me and I was alone, I wouldn't stand a chance in hell. The first time we couldn't prevent our transformation. It happened, whether or not we wanted it to, when the moon dictated it would happen. The only thing I could control was where I was when it happened.

"Okay. I'll go back to Wolford. But I'm not going to accept you as my mate."

He squeezed my hands. "Hayden—"

"No. I'm not comfortable with it."

"You have to have someone. If not me, then select someone else."

Strangely, I suddenly couldn't imagine anyone else I'd rather be with. Not that I was going to confess that realization. Instead I just said, "Let's see what happens when we get to Wolford."

"Fair enough."

We sat there for several long, silent moments just holding hands. Finally I worked myself free of his grasp and forced myself to my feet. "We're throwing a party here tonight after work. It was Lisa's idea. Kind of an end-to-winter-break thing."

"Am I invited?"

My voice was hoarse when I said, "Yeah."

As I left him there and made my way back to my room, all I could do was hope that leaving with him—and not trying to run away again—would turn out to be the right decision.

SEVEN

My last day at the resort was uneventful. Daniel was gone from the condo when I got up, and although I couldn't see him, I felt him watching me—as I walked to work, as I trudged home. A tiny part of me wished he'd join me as I made my way through the snow. Part of me was glad for the distance between us, until I realized that it almost made tonight seem like a date.

Still, I couldn't describe the anticipation rushing through me as I got ready for the party. Or the insecurity.

"Be still," Lisa commanded.

"But I want to see."

"When I'm finished."

She was applying makeup to my face. I'd practiced a little with the girls at school but had never quite mastered the skill.

"You won't make me look like a clown, will you?" I asked.

Lisa growled, and if I hadn't known better, I'd have thought she was a Shifter.

"Relax. Just relax. I was the makeup artist for all my high school productions. I practically live at Sephora."

She said that as though it was supposed to mean something to me.

Leaning back, she studied me for a second. "You don't even know what I'm talking about, do you? Did you escape from some religious commune or something?"

"No."

"Daniel—is he taking you back? Do you need help?"

I grabbed her hand. It was so much easier when I knew no emotions would blast through me. "I'm fine. I just grew up in a small town, went to a girls' boarding school, have never really flourished in the dating scene, that's all."

"Okay, if you say so. But Daniel really likes you." She moved in toward me, and I stopped her with a hand to her shoulder.

"How do you know that?"

"Duh? The way he looks at you."

"Exactly how?"

"It's just so intense. Like you mean everything to him. Like he can't stand the thought of a minute without you. And tonight he is really not going to be able to take his eyes off you." She spun me around to face the mirror.

I gawked at my reflection and slowly came off the stool. She'd taken scissors to my hair to create wispy bangs. I couldn't tell that she'd put on makeup, but my caramel-shaded eyes were larger, luminescent, exotic. She'd somehow enhanced their oval shape. My lips looked fuller. Definitely kissable.

The thought made me grow warm, and I watched as a blush crept over my chin and rose into my cheeks. It probably started at my stomach, but since I was wearing a heavy cowl-necked sweater that draped off one shoulder, it was difficult to tell. The sweater was a deep purple that made my hair appear blonder, my eyes a richer hue.

"It doesn't look like me," I said in awe.

"Of course it does," she said, brushing off my concerns. "And wait until Daniel gets a good look at you. He's going to be stunned speechless."

Lisa called that right.

In spite of the frigid winter air we had the front door and the French doors that led to the deck propped open so people could wander in and out. The lights were dimmed low and pine-scented candles flickered around the rooms. Music was playing. We'd moved all the furniture from the center of the living room so there was plenty of space to dance. Some people lounged on the sofa, love seats, or chairs lined along the walls. Some used floor pillows. We had snacks, sodas, and beers. No one was around to card anyone, so I grabbed a bottle and gulped some of the bitter brew. I was nervous, waiting for Daniel to show up.

Wiping my hands on my jeans, I regretted that I'd run into a store on my afternoon break and bought a pair of spike-heeled boots. They were impractical, and I didn't know when I'd ever have a chance to wear them again. But they made me feel elegant, even if my feet were killing me. I thought they made my legs look long and slender. Especially by the time I'd finished my first beer and gone for a second.

I was in the bathroom, where we'd poured tons of ice into the tub to use as our cooler. I'd just pulled out the bottle when one of the guys I'd worked with during the past month, Mark, came up to me, snaked his hand around my waist, snuggled me against his side, and cupped my bottom. "Don't you look great?"

I could tell by the slight slurring of his words and the way he swayed that he'd already had too much to drink.

I also knew he was harmless. Before I could extricate myself from his hold and get his hand off my butt, a low, warning growl echoed off the walls.

Mark released me and spun around so fast that he almost toppled over. Regaining his balance, he asked, "Dude, was that you?"

I wasn't surprised to see Daniel standing in the doorway. What did surprise me was how glad I was to see him. He appeared menacing, and at that precise moment he left no doubt that he was defending his territory—which was me.

I was torn between being offended at the old-fashioned gesture and flattered by his determination. He looked great. He'd obviously shaved. He was wearing a black cashmere pullover, and the emerald in his eyes glowed.

Into the silence permeating the bathroom Mark said, "You want a beer?"

Only then did Daniel shift his gaze to me. His eyes widened slightly as though he was surprised by my appearance, and I realized he'd probably tracked me through the condo by scent alone. Only now was he getting a good look at me. His nostrils flared; his eyes heated. I couldn't prevent the little thrill of pleasure that shot through me.

Mark held up his hands, like someone warding off an

angry mob. "I didn't realize she was taken."

"I wasn't," I felt compelled to tell him. "I'm not," I added for Daniel's benefit.

"Yeah, well. I'm not here for trouble, just a good time." Mark grabbed a beer and edged his way past Daniel in order to get out of the room.

"That was kinda rude," I said testily.

"What'd you do to yourself?"

"You don't like it?"

He angled his head to study me better. "I like it. But I liked you the other way, too."

"So tomorrow I'll go back to the other way." I flicked my fingers through my bangs. "Well, except for the hair. Beer?"

He wandered into the small room and snatched a beer from the tub. He jerked his head toward the door. "You like that guy?"

I shrugged. "Yeah. He's nice."

Daniel scowled fiercely, and I realized there was nothing he did that wasn't predatory. "I mean, more than like," he said.

"You said like."

He sighed with impatience, and I found myself enjoying the moment, realizing in spite of all his insistence that he would be my mate, he wasn't quite comfortable with the emotions that came along with the declaration. I thought it was cute.

"That other *L*-word," he muttered.

"Lycanthropy?" I whispered.

"Funny."

I relented. "I don't love him, if that's what you're asking. I barely know him."

His gaze dropped to my hip. "Sure looked like he thought he knew you."

"He was just being friendly. He's really harmless." *Unlike you*, I almost added.

He narrowed his eyes, looked as though he was going to argue. Instead he twisted the top of his beer, took a swig, then studied me. "You shouldn't flirt with other guys."

"Why? Because I belong to you?"

"Because you need someone who can protect you and that guy can't. But I will."

Two other people edged their way into the bathroom, grabbed some bottles, and went out.

"Come on," I said. "I don't intend to spend my party in the bathroom."

I walked into the hallway with Daniel right on my heels. Music was blasting in the dimly lit living room. People were gyrating on the floor.

"Do you dance?" Daniel asked beside my ear, his breath skimming over my neck and sending a warm tingle of pleasure down my spine.

How could he make me feel things with so little effort? I shook my head.

He took my bottle and set it on a small nearby table along with his. Then he grabbed my hand and began tugging me toward the makeshift dance floor. I dug in the heels of my expensive boots.

"No!" I shook my head, laughing. "I'll just make a fool of myself."

He leaned in. "You won't see these people after tonight. What does it matter? Besides, I thought you wanted to party. What better way than with a little wildness?"

What he said was true, but I'd never danced before. Had never been to a dance. While I'd watched people at Out of Bounds, I'd never joined them.

"You just move your body around. No big deal. This isn't *Dancing with the Stars*," he said.

"Promise not to laugh?" I asked.

He made a cross over his heart and dragged me onto the dance floor. The beer I'd had earlier definitely released some of my inhibitions, but still I glanced around.

"Don't look at them," Daniel said. "Just look at me."

Gracefully, smoothly, he was moving in rhythm with the music. I found myself following his lead. It was so easy. And so much fun. I smiled. I laughed. I'd missed

112

out on this. Our biggest celebrations at Wolford occurred during the summer and winter solstices, when as many families as possible came to celebrate the existence of our kind. There were games, music, dancing. I'd tried to mingle, but mostly I'd just watched. My kind didn't mean to be cruel, but they all knew of my abilities and weren't comfortable around me. Not that I blamed them. When the emotions bombarding me got to be too much, I'd go into the basement and read a book in a little nook I'd created for myself. I wasn't completely protected there, but only the most intense emotions would reach me.

The worst emotions of all had been my own when I was there. The loneliness. The isolation. I always preferred being at school, being around Statics. But there were things I couldn't share with them, which also created a sense of not truly belonging.

But tonight I was happy. I was dancing. I was with people. So many people. There had to be at least a hundred people here. The winter workers, the college students who would head back to their universities tomorrow so they could start class Monday. I wanted to go with them, wherever they'd be traveling. Instead I'd be heading back to Wolford with Daniel.

He grabbed my hand, pulled me toward him. "Don't think about it!" he yelled in my ear above the music. After spinning me around, he set me back away from him so we could resume our dancing.

"How did you know?" I yelled. How did he know what I was thinking?

I was pretty sure he heard me, but he ignored me, moving with the music—which suddenly stopped. People yelled, moaned, groaned. A couple of guys yelled obscenities. A slow song started up. Joyous shouts and clapping echoed through the room.

Before I could make a hasty exit from the dance area, Daniel had pulled me into his arms.

"I've never—" I began.

"Just relax into it, Hayden."

He put my arms around his neck and wound his around my waist. We weren't really dancing. Just moving our feet. But it was nice. So nice. To be this close to another Shifter, to not feel his emotions, to only be distracted by mine. And they were darting all over the place. Contentment, quickly followed by that sense of fright again because what I felt I felt so strongly. I was loving this moment with Daniel. I didn't even have to pretend I was normal. For these few moments I truly was.

I nestled my face in the nook of his shoulder, grateful I'd spent so much of my hard-earned money on these boots that made me tall enough to fit so perfectly against him. "How did you know I was thinking about going back to Wolford?" I asked quietly. "Are you a mind reader?"

"You stopped smiling."

"I never smile there. Please don't take me back, Daniel."

"I have to, Hayden." He lowered his head, his breath skimming along the sensitive skin just below my ear. "I couldn't stand it if anything happened to you. I truly believe that it's the only place where you'll be safe."

Until that moment it hadn't occurred to me that maybe taking me back to Wolford wasn't any easier for him than going was for me. I could continue to be difficult, to search for ways to escape. Or I could accept the inevitable as I'd told him I would last night.

I felt the lingering remnants of a fight seep out of me as I truly accepted my decision to return to our secret sanctuary. My body relaxed against Daniel's. His arms closed more tightly around me, drawing me nearer.

"Thank you," he whispered.

I wondered if he knew what I did—that everything would change once we returned to Wolford. That I would change. That the emotions of others constantly slamming into me would wear me down. That I would know no peace. Then my full moon would arrive. . . .

He wanted me to have faith that everything would be all right. But all I was sure of was that I had tonight. So I held on tightly. I didn't flinch when people bumped into me. I let the music flow through me. I listened to the din of conversation. A cacophony of sounds surrounded me but they were all outside of me. Inside of me I knew only my thoughts, experienced only my emotions. While they were a little scary—because I was enjoying so much being within the circle of Daniel's arms—they were also so totally amazing. Because they were mine and mine alone.

The slow music had barely drifted away before a louder, faster beat was thumping through the room. People separated and returned to more enthusiastic dancing.

Daniel took my hand and we threaded our way through the crowd to the French doors. We didn't stop on the deck, but he led me down the stairs, our feet crunching on the snow. The heeled boots were really difficult to maneuver in as we crossed the drifts. The moonlight cast a blue haze over everything. For just a moment I wondered if it was possible to defeat the harvester, but then all thoughts—except for those centered around Daniel—left my mind as he brought me around to face him.

"All the insanity and craziness in there, all the noise, is that what it's like for you when the Shifters' emotions are hitting you?" he asked, his gaze latched on to mine.

"Not exactly but it's probably the closest way to describe it. It's not noise, but it's overwhelming and chaotic. It's mostly mental but physical, too, because I can't help but respond to what I'm feeling." I shook my head. "It's impossible to describe."

While the music drifted out from the condo, it was too far away to be bothersome. The snap of a twig or branch—probably weighted down by snow—broke through the stillness. An owl hooted.

I hadn't grabbed my jacket before coming out here. I should have been shivering with the cold. But I wasn't. All I seemed able to manage was to stare into Daniel's eyes and to welcome the warmth emanating from his body.

He cupped my face with both his hands. The pads of his palms were heated, rough, and callused. Where once I had been suspicious of him because I couldn't feel his emotions, now I relished the fact that when he touched me like this, the emotions that stirred within me were mine and mine alone.

"I'm not going to let anything happen to you," he said quietly, fiercely.

His lips touched the corner of my mouth, and desire spiked through me. I turned my head into the kiss, to meet his lips as they skimmed over mine, before returning to settle firmly into place. Winter faded away, and it was as if I'd stepped into the middle of summer. Heat consumed me as passion rose up and swirled through me.

This kiss was different from the one he'd given me on

the ski lift. That one had been tentative, a testing, a need for closeness to celebrate what we'd accomplished. This one was more, so much more. I'd never dared hope that I could experience something so intimate with a Shifter without being destroyed by it. But even as inexperienced as I was, I knew no other kiss would have been as thrilling, as satisfying, as marvelous.

When Daniel drew back, I looked deep into his eyes, became as lost in them as I had in the kiss. For the first time since I'd initially spotted him, I truly wanted to leave with him.

He stroked his thumb over my lips. They were sensitive, damp, and swollen.

"Say your good-byes. We leave just before sunrise."

With that he released his hold on me and disappeared between the trees, into the forest. He wasn't sleeping on the couch tonight, and I wondered if it was because he feared the temptation to ascend the stairs would be too great. I didn't want to feel this closeness to him, and yet I couldn't deny the wonder of it. I didn't want to contemplate that perhaps he could be my mate. I'd never before felt this deep yearning. I'd never before welcomed the nearness of a Shifter more than the nearness of a Static.

The warmth I'd felt with his nearness dissipated, and the cold swept in. I released a hard shiver, wrapped my arms around myself, and scurried back to the condo.

To enjoy my last hours of peace before beginning the journey that would see me either victorious standing beneath a full moon—or dead.

EIGHT

I didn't sleep. Instead I just lay in my bed and watched the shadows dancing over my ceiling as the moonlight played around the room. When I was with Daniel, returning to Wolford seemed like the right decision. When I wasn't with him, it seemed foolhardy. Just as he'd promised that he wouldn't let anything happen to me, I was just as determined to ensure that nothing would happen to him. No matter what it required. I didn't want him or any other Shifter to perish on my behalf.

I welcomed the first hint of an approaching dawn with a sense of anticipation . . . and dread.

Daniel hadn't given me a precise time to meet him,

but somehow I sensed his arrival.

I got out of bed and crept to the window. Peering out, I saw him at the edge of the tree line, sitting on my silent snowmobile. The roads leading into the national forest would be closed to vehicles. With indirect routes we could get there traveling over the snow.

In truth I probably should have kept going until I reached an ocean or another country. Instead I'd reached Athena and decided to stop for a while, to earn some money, get my bearings, and make plans for where to go next. I didn't think I would have decided to return to Wolford. But that's where I was going.

A light snowfall had begun. The sooner we left, the better.

With determination to get on with it, to face whatever had to be faced, I moved away from the window and pulled on my clothes: jeans, T-shirt, sweater, jacket, gloves, hat, and boots. Everything else I needed was stuffed into my backpack.

I hadn't said good-bye to anyone, hadn't told anyone I was leaving. It would have been too difficult, might have required explanations and assurances. I knew everyone would understand. Athena was a place where friendships as temporary as the snow made their home. The majority of the people who were here now would be gone within the next few days. The thought made me feel not quite so different.

I slung my backpack over my shoulder and headed down the stairs. On the kitchen table I left the note I'd written: *Heading back home. Thanks for everything.*

Thanks for keeping your emotions to yourself, I'd thought but not written. The neatly printed words seemed inadequate, but I had nothing else of myself to leave behind. I slipped onto the deck, locking the door behind me. The moon had begun its descent, so it was darker now than it had been when I'd come outside with Daniel the evening before. I could see only the outline of his silhouette and distant lights from the street reflecting off the snowmobile. His determination to protect me, even with risk to himself, touched me deeply. But it wasn't what I wanted. I didn't want anyone sacrificing themselves for me.

Maybe I shouldn't have run from Wolford. Maybe I should have expressed my concerns to the elders. But that night I'd been shaken and terrified. Escape had been the only thought running through my head. I still wasn't sure going back was the right thing to do. But I'd give it a chance.

I could see paw prints circling around, moving in and out among the trees. Daniel no doubt, keeping vigil all night. I wondered why he'd felt the need last night and not before. Maybe he'd expected me to make a final break for it. I was glad the snow drifting down would cover the evidence of his prowling. I didn't want anyone to grab a rifle and go searching for whatever had made the prints.

He didn't say anything as I approached. What was there to say?

He started the snowmobile as I swung my leg over the seat and settled in behind him. Wrapping my arms around his waist, I pressed my cheek to his back. As we launched forward, I fought not to look back.

But nostalgia got the better of me. I watched a place where I'd been happy and safe disappear behind a curtain of snow and distance.

We traveled until long after nightfall. With the first shift came the ability to see at night. Even in human form we retained some of our animal tendencies. While the snowmobile had headlights, I knew Daniel was relying more on his instincts to cut around trees and avoid rocks or mounds of snow that might be hiding some hazard.

We'd stopped three times throughout the day at little out-of-the-way gas stations to refuel the snowmobile. I'd made use of the restroom and grabbed snacks and beverages. We were taking a trail that led through the wilderness into the national forest. We weren't going to run across any small towns or other evidence of civilization. I didn't doubt for a minute that Daniel could provide for us, but it wouldn't be my preferred diet so I indulged when I could.

The moon had risen high in the black sky when Daniel finally brought us to a stop in a small clearing. I slid off the back of the bike, stretched my cramped muscles, and inhaled deeply. I could smell the sharp tang of evergreens.

I watched as Daniel dragged to the middle of the clearing the bundle of supplies that had been strapped to the snowmobile. "I've never been camping," I confessed, "so you're going to have to tell me what to do."

"You've never been camping? What about when you ran off?"

"Just kept going until I reached Athena."

"Do you know how dangerous that was? How many accidents happen because people fall asleep—"

"I'm not in the mood for a lecture about what I should have done. How can I help?"

He located a large flashlight. After turning it on, he handed it to me. "Keep the beam directed where I'm working."

I knew he probably didn't need the light, but I found it comforting. He began digging through the snow to get to the ground. I knew he was making preparations for a campfire.

"Wouldn't you be able to dig more quickly if you

shifted? You know? Use those paws to burrow down to the earth?"

He glanced up and grinned. "But then I'd have to shift back to take care of everything else. Besides, I'm making progress."

I studied him as he made short work of clearing an area of snow—as though he needed to prove that he was as capable in human form as in wolf form. While I was feeling pretty useless.

"If you don't need the flashlight to finish setting up camp, I'll go find us some wood."

Standing, he dusted the snow off his gloves and clothes. "Don't go far."

"If I was planning to make a break for it, I'd have been gone before you showed up this morning." Without waiting for him to reply, I headed toward the trees. A lot of dead branches were still attached to trunks. I snapped them off until I had a good armload, then I carried them back to our camp.

The bundle of supplies was now resting open in the snow. Daniel stopped working on the tent and helped me arrange the wood in our little pit. His movements were sure, confident. The quiet around us was interrupted with a crackle as the first sparks began to take hold.

"There," he said, unfolding his body and dusting off his hands again. "That should get going and warm us up."

I placed my hands toward the emerging flames. The air was crisp with cold, and the heat from the fire was reaching out to me. "I guess working as a forest guide you do a lot of camping."

"Pretty much every night last summer."

We worked together to finish putting up the small tent. It would hold one person comfortably. Two, not so much. I wondered if he was planning to keep watch.

From the bundle he'd carted over earlier, he grabbed a bag and brought it over to the campfire, which was now roaring. He set out a plastic tarp. I dropped onto it. He reached back into the bag.

"So what'll it be?" he asked, holding up a can. "Vegetable soup?" He held up another can. "Or vegetable stew?"

I laughed. "Stew."

Before long I was drinking the stew from a mug that we'd use later for coffee or tea or hot chocolate. The wind had begun to pick up, whistling through the trees.

"So . . . did you have a mate . . . before you left Seattle?" I asked.

"No." He peered over at me as though unsure about how much to reveal. "I dated," he continued, "but there was no one who ever struck me as the *one*."

"So no tattoo."

Again a slight hesitation. "I have a tattoo."

"What? Just for fun?"

"It means something to me."

"What's it mean?"

"My search, I guess, my search for someplace to belong. It starts at the back of my shoulder, goes down my bicep." He touched his right arm, as though he could feel it through his clothes.

I wondered if he'd ever share it with me. Strange how much I wanted him to, even though I was *not* going to accept him as my mate. I felt a need to fill in the silence stretching between us. "So you're in college?" I slapped my forehead. "Ugh. I can't believe I asked that."

He grinned. "What? Why?"

I smiled at him. "It's like the number one question I got asked in Athena whenever a new group of students arrived for winter break. It always seemed so unoriginal."

"It's a good question, though. Yeah, I go to college. I want to get into law enforcement at some point."

Shifters often lived and worked among the Statics, but even then we had our little pockets of society. Yet Wolford was recognized as our main hub. It was where those who had first come to America had settled. It was a place that all Shifters could call home, even if they'd never been there.

"Guess this isn't how you wanted to spend your winter

break," I said, feeling a little guilty that my running away may have ruined whatever plans he'd had.

"I didn't have any plans," he said as if reading my mind, and I realized he was much better at figuring me out than I was at guessing what he thought or felt. "Although I'm thinking of taking up bungee jumping next winter."

I laughed, remembering my comment to him that first night about bungee jumping. "Yeah, well, don't expect me to join you." I realized we were talking as though we'd both be around next winter. As though everything would turn out okay. "Back at Athena I kept feeling like I was being watched." Before he could answer, I said, "And not by you. I always felt a pleasant sensation when you were watching me. This other feeling I got . . . it wasn't pleasant at all."

"I didn't notice anything when I was looking around."

I nodded again. "I'm probably just paranoid."

"Under your circumstances I would be, too."

"I wonder why now? How it found us?"

He placed another log on the fire. "If you keep thinking about it, you're not going to be able to sleep."

"I doubt I'll be able to sleep anyway. Like I told you this is my first time camping. It's nice out here, but it's also kinda creepy. I mean, it's just us. I feel sorta small, insignificant."

"How could you have never gone camping?"

"I was never a guide. When I was at Wolford, I stayed in the manor. And at the boarding school the girls were more into pajama parties than roughing it out in the wilderness." I drew my legs up and wrapped my arms around them. "Don't get me wrong. I enjoy the outdoors. But"—I glanced back at the tent—"if a bear shows up, that's not a lot of protection."

"You're safe. Bears hibernate in winter."

"Okay, then, a cougar. I know they're around. I heard one attacked a Dark Guardian last summer."

"Yeah, Rafe, I think. But you don't have to worry about it. That's what I'm here for." He leaned in, his eyes warming me as much as our fire, his full lips parted slightly, his gaze roaming over my face as though he intended to memorize every curve and line. "As for your observation that there are only the two of us—I kinda like that."

Then his mouth covered mine.

All thought was eclipsed by the hunger of his kiss. It was as though he'd never be satisfied, he'd always want more—or maybe those were my feelings, my thoughts. What I did know, without a doubt, was that he drew me in, made me crave more than my solitary existence, made me want these wonderful feelings and sensations.

Drawing back, breathing heavily, he pressed his

forehead to mine. "You say you won't accept me as your mate, but you never push me away when I kiss you."

I could barely think when he kissed me. How was I supposed to set up defenses and push him away?

"You confuse me. Daniel"—I shook my head, trying to clear it—"I don't want to, but I like you."

"That's a start."

"This is such a bad idea." Such a bad idea. Whenever I was at Wolford, I would feel Shifters falling in love. I would experience the tenderness, the excitement, the yearning. Through others I understood the power of affection, how it made them alter priorities, lose sight of goals. How nothing mattered more than the person who was loved. It had always made me feel so incredibly alone. Had left me wanting so badly to be accepted by a guy for what I was: a Shifter with empathic abilities. I'd believed no human could ever accept all that I was. I'd feared no Shifter would either. And here I was beginning to feel as if I belonged—belonged with Daniel. I couldn't afford to care for him this deeply. *He* couldn't afford for me to care for him this deeply. I had to resist the temptation, the lure of accepting him as my mate. Of wanting to bond with him when my full moon arrived.

"I'm really tired," I said. "Tomorrow's going to be another long day. I should go to bed."

He leaned back to study me more closely, to judge the

truth of my words, maybe. I recognized the hurt of rejection in his eyes at my abrupt topic change. Quickly his emotions changed, became unreadable, as he returned to protector mode, putting his duty above his heart. His first duty was to get me back to Wolford at the elders' request.

"Yeah, you should," he said. Abruptly he got to his feet. Without him there, I swayed slightly, threw out my arm to save myself from face-planting in the snow.

"You sleep in the tent," he ordered. "I'm going to keep watch."

It hurt to hear his voice so flat, absent of even the faintest glimmer of teasing.

"Daniel—" ·

"You should hurry. I can feel a storm coming in on the wind."

Only then did I notice that the wind had picked up and that snow had begun falling again. I thought there was probably something I should say, but anything would be inadequate. I unfolded my legs and stood. "You want things I can't give you."

"You don't know what I want because you can't feel my emotions."

I couldn't experience them inside me, but I was discovering that I was still aware of what they were. "Good night, then."

I slipped into the tent but didn't zip it all the way closed. I left a small peephole. I watched him bank the fire. When he was finished, he strode to the edge of the camp, to the shadows. I could see only his silhouette, but I knew he was removing his clothes. Then he ran into the forest.

I waited for him to return. I was still waiting when sleep overcame me.

NINE

I awoke with a start. I lay still, listening to the sounds of the forest. Because of the moonlight dancing over the top of the tent, I knew it was still night. I didn't know what had disturbed my slumber. Then I heard a howl, a lonesome baying at the moon.

I wondered if it was Daniel.

The howl came again. For all I knew it was a real wolf. But if it was Daniel and I just happened to be out taking a stroll and our paths crossed—

Throwing back the top of the sleeping bag, I grabbed my fur-lined walking boots and pulled them on. I shoved my arms into my jacket and pulled my knitted cap low.

After scooting over to the tent opening, I peered through the small hole I hadn't zipped all the way earlier. The fire was nothing except smoldering embers. The site appeared deserted. I snatched my flashlight from my backpack, unzipped the tent opening, and crawled out.

Crouched, my arms wrapped around my knees, I remained still and listened. With my first transformation all my senses would become more acute. I'd noticed as I got closer to my full moon that some of my senses were becoming more acute, but they still fell far short of what they'd eventually be.

There was a stillness to the night that reminded me of the way Daniel sat in the chocolate shop. Awaiting something. A calm before the storm.

The air was crisp, with a biting chill. The snow was falling lightly. The wind kicked up and died and kicked up again, as though it couldn't quite decide what it wanted to do. A little like me where Daniel was concerned. I could see his clothes still resting where he'd discarded them earlier, now dusted with snow. So he was still out on the prowl.

Maybe it *was* his howl I'd heard.

The trees awash in moonlight were gorgeous. The landscape had a romantic feel to it. The kind that demanded exploring, I thought, as I shoved myself to my feet.

And with any luck maybe I'd run into Daniel, catch a glimpse of him in wolf form. Unfortunately enough snow had fallen and wind had swirled to erase his tracks. I didn't yet have the ability to follow by scent. But I headed off in the direction that I'd seen him take earlier.

By now he'd probably circled around, returned to camp a couple of times, and gone back out on the hunt. I had little doubt he was searching for meat. It was more difficult to locate in winter, but I knew he'd find it. Funny how after only a few days I had absolute faith in his survival skills.

The only real sound I heard was my footsteps sloshing through the snow and my breath as the force of it increased with my movements.

As I eased between two evergreens, I came up short at the sight of a big black cat several yards away. A panther. Emitting a low, deep purr, it was rubbing its shoulder against the bark of a tree. It reminded me of how I'd stretched languorously and sighed when I'd splurged and gotten a hot stone massage at the spa in Athena.

The panther was facing away from me so it hadn't yet picked up my scent. I'd read somewhere that panthers were really leopards without their spots. But in North America leopards existed only in zoos. So where had this one come from?

It was so large and muscular that it had to be fully

grown. Had it once been someone's exotic pet that had been set free? Were there others in this area?

I knew there were mountain lions and cougars in the woods near Wolford, but I'd never heard of a black one, so I thought this was a real panther. Shifters weren't exactly on friendly terms with cougars. I didn't know if they were natural enemies of wolves, but I knew that our scent was slightly different from a real wolf and that cougars tended to attack Shifters.

I didn't know how a panther would react. I was half tempted to approach it, remove my glove, and pet it, just run my fingers through the fur that reflected the moonlight dancing between the branches. But I knew they were predators and meat eaters. And I knew better than to approach a wild animal.

Suddenly it whipped its head around. It was too far away for me to see its eyes clearly, but I felt them locked on me. The panther went low to the ground, growled deep in its throat, and bared its sharp incisors.

Everything within me stilled. Crap. Where was Daniel? Would he be able to sense that I might be in danger? Strange that I didn't doubt for one second that he could take this cat on.

Suddenly it sprinted away, its movements lithe and smooth. It was incredibly gorgeous.

Taking a deep breath, feeling weak in the knees, I pressed my back to a tree. Wow. That was close. He could have just as easily come in my direction. I considered yelling out for Daniel. I was fairly certain that he wouldn't go too far from camp. Not if he was keeping watch over me. So where was he?

It had been stupid to try to find him when there were no tracks to go by and the weather was kicking up. I shoved myself away from the tree and began retracing the path I'd taken.

When I got back to camp, Daniel was there, crouched beside the fire that he'd obviously restarted. He snapped his head in my direction and scowled. "What are you doing out wandering around?"

I knelt beside him, enjoying the warmth generated by the flames. "I thought I heard you howling. I went looking for you."

"Do you know how dangerous that is?"

"No kidding. I ran into a panther."

"In these woods?"

He seemed as surprised by the revelation as I'd been. "I know. Crazy, huh? I wonder how he came to be here."

"People sometimes buy wild animals as pets. Then when they discover they weren't meant to be tamed, they set them free."

"Yeah, that's what I was thinking. It was so gorgeous."

"Were you afraid of it?"

"Not really afraid. Wary, maybe. I mean, it was the

last thing I expected to see." I glanced around. I could see that the sky was beginning to lighten. I hadn't realized I'd woken up so close to dawn. "When I stepped out of the tent, it was so amazing, with the snow falling and the swirling wind"—both had now died down—"that I just wanted to explore for a bit. Knowing what I'm going to face, how frightening it's going to be . . . I appreciate everything else a little more."

I didn't mean to be macabre or to sound as though I'd given up. I hadn't. But the thought lingered in the corner of my mind that no matter how much I wanted to survive everything that awaited me with the next full moon, the outcome might not be anything I could control.

"You're not going through it alone, Hayden."

I wanted to hug him, snuggle up against him, but it was best if I didn't give him any sort of encouragement. "I'll never accept you as my mate."

"That won't stop me from being there."

"Why? Why are you so insistent—"

He touched his thumb to my lips, silencing me. Looking into his eyes, I imagined I could see into the depths of his soul.

"Because I care about you," he said quietly. Wrapping his hand around the nape of my neck, holding me steady, he leaned in and kissed me.

I didn't pull back. I didn't tell him not to. I just let it

happen. With his lips on mine the fears and worries were swept away. I knew they'd return, stronger and more powerful, but for this brief space of time, I relished the fact that a Shifter, a Dark Guardian, cared for me.

I had the one thing I'd always wanted. But I knew I wouldn't be able to hold on to him. That in the end I'd have to betray him and everything he felt for me.

TEN

I found it strange, two days later, when we crossed over into our national forest, that I recognized it. I hadn't expected really to notice. Forests, woods, mountains—even covered in snow—had their own personalities, their own characteristics that distinguished them from others.

I tightened my hold on Daniel. We'd been fortunate that we'd been able to travel over the snow and find the occasional gas station or small town where we could stock up on supplies. I figured he'd marked the route when he'd come after me.

I squeezed my eyes shut and tried to put up barriers. We'd be there soon.

It was near nightfall the next day when Daniel gunned the throttle and swung the vehicle around, causing snow to erupt around us. I released a small squeal and clung to him more fiercely. He came to a stop and cut the engine.

I never knew silence could be so loud. It was a strange thing to think: how could silence be anything except quiet—but the suddenness of it was almost deafening.

"Are you sensing anyone's emotions other than your own?" Daniel asked.

"Not yet."

"We'll be there later tonight. Are you ready for this?"

"As ready as I'll ever be."

It was nearing three in the morning when we finally arrived at the wrought iron gate. A fence surrounded our hidden compound. Little sparks of emotion darted in and out of me. Nothing intense, nothing overwhelming, just the vigilance of the Dark Guardians who were patrolling the area. No outsiders ever stumbled upon us here, because the Dark Guardians were vigilant about keeping them at a distance—although I sometimes suspected that a layer of magic shielded us as well.

The elders held a lot of secrets.

Daniel swiped a keycard, and the gate slowly began to open, beckoning us in. We were a strange combination of magic and technology. Then we were riding toward the monstrous manor where the elders resided year-round, where I had escaped from only a few short weeks ago.

Daniel brought the snowmobile to a halt near the building and turned it off. I was hit by the silence. I heard an owl hoot in the distance and farther off the howl of a wolf. Faint light was spilling out onto the snow through a few of the downstairs windows. It created a peaceful illusion, something an artist might capture on canvas. I wished I could believe what it was offering.

I eased off the seat. My legs were rubbery from the long journey—or at least that's what I blamed the sensation on as they started to buckle. Daniel's arm whipped out and wrapped around me, drawing me in, holding me up.

"Whoa," he said. "You okay?"

"Yeah."

"Are you feeling—"

"No." I touched his roughened cheek. I liked it when he didn't shave. It made him look menacing, tough, and sexy. "Don't worry. I'll be okay."

With his arm still around me, he led me up the steps and opened the door. As I walked through it into the foyer, I saw that a few of the Dark Guardians were waiting.

Emotions swirled into me, intense, but soft, warm, and welcoming.

"We heard you arrive," Lucas, leader of the Dark Guardians, said. Like Daniel he was tall and broad. His hair was a mixture of black, brown, and gray, which made him easy to spot in wolf form when I saw him patrolling the grounds.

"Sorry," Daniel said. "Guess we should have walked from the gate."

"Probably wouldn't have mattered," Kayla said. She was Lucas's mate, had joined our group last summer. Her hair was the red coloring of a fox more than a wolf, but when she shifted, she was striking. "We were sleeping light."

She took a step toward me and tentatively wrapped her arms around me. "Welcome home."

Her emotions burst into me, but it wasn't a hard hit. It was like fireworks erupting in the sky. She'd been worried about me, and now those fears were fading away to be replaced with relief. Joy.

They made my throat clog with my own emotions. I'd lived on the fringe, spending most of my time at the boarding school, and it had never occurred to me that they'd miss me here, that they'd worry about me. Part of me had even thought they'd be glad that the freak— the one who stopped their emotions from being private— wasn't around.

"My turn," Lindsey said. Her blond hair was almost

white. Last summer I'd experienced her inner turmoil as she struggled with her feelings for both Connor and Rafe. Dark, brooding Rafe stood just behind her. After she'd chosen him, they were never far apart. When she hugged me, her true gladness swept through me. I hadn't expected it. It weakened my knees.

"I'm not a hugger," Brittany muttered, "but Connor and I are glad you're back." She and Connor were a contrast: Brittany with her black hair, Connor with his blond.

"The elders will want to talk with you in the morning," Lucas said, "but for now you should probably try to get some sleep."

I nodded, too weary to object.

"Since my emotions don't bother you," Brittany said, "we thought you could share a room with me."

"I have a room," I reminded her. I used it whenever I was here.

"Yeah, but do you want to sleep alone?"

I didn't. My gaze darted to Daniel. I was surprised by how much I wanted him sleeping with me, holding me. But I knew the elders would never go for that. They were very strict about who could share a room. Girls and guys were segregated.

"Okay. Yeah. Sure." There was so much I wanted to say to Daniel. But it was personal, private. I wanted a moment alone to talk with him, but as the girls guided me toward the grand sweeping stairs, I knew I wasn't going to get the chance. Maybe tomorrow.

I glanced over my shoulder. He was already deep in discussion with the guys, no doubt planning how best to protect me. I felt a spike of fury from the others and resolve. I was in for a roller-coaster ride of emotions. Everyone was right. I needed to sleep if I could, because I was going to be battered.

"Are our emotions bothering you now?" Lindsey asked.

"It's not too bad. I can sense that you're trying to keep them tamped down. I appreciate it."

"It would probably blow you away to know how excited we really are to have you back," Kayla said. "It would be awesome if you could block our emotions so we could hang out more."

We were at the top of the stairs. I came to a stop. "You want to hang out with me?"

"Why do you sound so surprised? This Shifter world is new to me. I don't have many friends. I'd love to have another, would love for it to be you."

Before last summer she hadn't even known we existed, certainly hadn't known she had the amazing ability to shift.

"Maybe," I said, not willing to commit. This was all

new to me. I could talk to elderly men . . . I could talk with Daniel. I could befriend the girls at school. Maybe it wouldn't be so hard to be friends with other Shifters. I'd enjoyed making friendships among Statics, even if they'd only been temporary.

I followed Brittany into her room. There were two beds. Some of my clothes were folded and set on one of them.

"I guess you all had faith in Daniel bringing me back," I said as she closed the door behind us.

"Sure."

I walked to the bed and found some flannel pants and a long-sleeved T-shirt among my things. I fingered the drawstring. "So . . . you spent some time with him last summer—when the elders tried to pair you up."

She sat on the bed and pulled her legs beneath her. "Yeah. We took a group of girls into the woods for their first campout."

"Did you ever see him shift?"

She furrowed her brow, shook her head. "No." She grinned. "So what's he look like? With his black hair he probably looks pretty menacing as a wolf."

"I've never actually seen him in wolf form."

Before she could comment, I slipped into the bathroom and turned on the shower. I stripped out of my clothes, stepped into the shower and welcomed the hot water sluicing over my body. I began to relax from the top of my head to the tips of my toes, imagining a waterfall cascading through me, washing away all the tension, as I'd done so often at the resort—

Fury plowed into me, nearly staggered me. I braced my hand on the tiled wall, bowed my head, and fought back. It had to be the guys, discussing the dangers, plotting how to destroy the harvester.

A brisk knock sounded on the door.

"Hayden, are you okay? I heard you cry out," shouted Brittany.

"I'm fine." Grabbing the towel, I staggered out of the shower, my motions jerky as I dried off. I pulled on my flannel pants and top. With my hair dripping, dampening my shirt, I grabbed the edge of the counter, surprised that the marble didn't dent from my grip.

A flurry of emotions whipped through me like a tornado. Concern. Anger. Pride. A need to control. Fear again. That awful bone-chilling terror.

The door burst open. Daniel stood there, everyone who'd greeted us in the entryway pushing against him, vying to see what was going on. So many emotions blasted me that I couldn't separate them. They swamped me, consumed me.

The room spun around. The floor and ceiling traded places. Everything slanted. The floor was suddenly within inches of hitting my nose.

Daniel scooped me up and cradled me against his broad chest.

"Everyone out!" he yelled. "Get as far away from her as you can."

"No," I said, clutching his shirt, trying to regain my strength. "There's fear, immense fear. Someone's being attacked, is in danger."

"Who?" Lucas asked.

"I don't know."

"One of the sentries," Connor remarked.

I heard the echo of pounding footsteps as everyone else rushed out. Daniel laid me on the bed.

I pressed my hands on either side of my head. "I can't help him. I don't want to feel this; I don't want to experience his death."

I was lost in the vortex of the thrill of transformation as the others shifted, the desperation to find the one in trouble, the determination to succeed.

I was barely aware of Daniel cradling my cheek. "Hayden, I don't know how to help you."

"Distract me; draw me away from their emotions."

His mouth landed on mine, tentatively at first and then with more force. I hated that his emotions couldn't pour into me and shove out all the others. All I could do was focus on the feel of his long body half covering mine, the strength in his hands as they skimmed down my sides and pressed me closer, the pliancy of his lips as they moved over mine, the velvety touch of his tongue swirling. . . .

Pleasure, like heated honey, poured over me, through me. I became lost in sensations so rich, so powerful that everything faded away, except my own emotions, my own desires.

When Daniel broke off the kiss, we both gasped, dragging in great gulps of air. I could see in his green gaze that powerful emotions were roiling through him. Although I couldn't exactly feel them, I could read them.

And they scared me a hell of a lot more than anything I'd ever felt before. He'd told me that he cared for me. But it was so much more than that.

He loved me.

ELEVEN

"It was the most hideous thing I'd ever seen," Seth said. "I've never wanted to shift so badly in my entire life."

"The fact that you didn't probably saved your life," Lucas told him. "It took guts to fight your instincts."

We were all in the front parlor. Only moments before, Brittany had burst into the bedroom to let us know that Seth—who'd been out on patrol—had encountered the harvester. All she'd seen was me sitting on the bed, my back against the headboard, and Daniel standing by the window looking out. After that heat-seeking kiss we'd untangled ourselves without a word and gone to our separate spaces. I didn't know what he'd seen in my eyes, but if it was anything like the desire I'd seen in his, then I figured he was probably as spooked as I was.

Although neither of us was as spooked as Seth. I was actually having some success at pushing back his emotions so they didn't consume me. I didn't want to invade his inner space, to share his feelings. He tried to mask the shaking of his hands by keeping them in motion, rubbing one and then the other.

"It must have heard you guys coming," he said, his voice warbling slightly.

Kayla and Lindsey walked in, both carrying trays with steaming mugs of hot chocolate that the cook had prepared.

"Here, hot chocolate for everyone," Kayla said, setting her tray on the coffee table in front of the sofa where Seth was sitting. I took one, finding I needed something to do with my hands as well, not because they were trembling, but because they wanted to touch Daniel.

Standing by the fireplace, he uncrossed his arms to take a mug from the tray that Lindsey offered him. The room seemed almost too warm with the large fire burning in the hearth, but I knew that Seth was still chilled from his encounter.

Seth peered up at the guys. They were all still standing, while the girls had settled into various chairs around the room. "You took a chance shifting."

"We didn't feel its presence," Lucas said. "We didn't smell it either. It smells like rotten eggs."

Seth turned up his nose. "It does. But I didn't smell it until it was already there. It was like it just materialized out of the ground."

"From hell," Connor said.

When everyone looked at him, he just shrugged. "That's where legend says it came from."

"He's right," I said. "Because of our healing properties, we're not easily killed. So it was created by black magic to destroy us. Or so says each of the ancient texts that I've read."

"I'm not a big believer in magic," Rafe said.

Connor looked at him as though he'd spoken in a foreign language. "Dude, you turn into a wolf."

"That's different. It's not spells and black cauldrons and eye of newt."

"Whatever," Brittany said. "Arguing about it isn't going to change the fact that we have one dangerous creature out there. Does anyone know if the elders have figured out how to destroy it?"

"With magic," came from the doorway, and we all turned to see the elders standing there.

"What kind of magic?" Rafe asked skeptically.

"We'll explain in the morning," Elder Wilde said. "It is still a few hours until light. You should all sleep now."

He held up a slender finger. "No shifting. The harvester can be anywhere."

"I thought the harvester had power only during the full moon," Lucas said.

"It is close enough to that time that it can begin to wreak havoc. The other elders and I will keep watch for the remainder of the night. The rest of you must sleep."

As I went up the stairs with the others, I thought it a little naïve to think any of us could sleep. I could feel Daniel's gaze on my back.

At the top of the stairs he said, "Hayden?"

I looked back and he jerked his head to the side. Touching Brittany's arm, I told her, "I'll be in the room in a minute."

I went over to Daniel and waited until everyone had disappeared down the hallway. He touched my cheek. "I won't let it have you."

I heard absolute conviction in his voice.

"You might not have a choice. You know as well as I do that the first shift is not controlled by the person but rather by the moon—there's no stopping it." Standing on my toes, I pressed a quick kiss to his lips.

Then I walked down the hallway. A jumble of emotions was going through me. And this time they were all mine.

TWELVE

After breakfast the next morning we all gathered in the council room. At a large round table sat the eight Dark Guardians—including Daniel—who remained at Wolford and the three elders. Elder Wilde was in the middle with Elder Thomas on one side of him and Elder Mitchell on the other. Normally before a Guardian experienced her first full moon, she was considered a novice and sat in a chair along the side of the room. But since this meeting came about because of me, I found myself sitting beside Elder Thomas, who held my hand with his gnarled one. After more than a hundred years of shifting, in spite of a Shifter's healing abilities, his body had begun to show the price of shaping and reshaping bones and muscles.

As leader of the Dark Guardians, Lucas stood. "As you know, the harvester threatened Hayden. It would not only reap her soul and her ability to shift, but her ability to sense others' emotions. We've identified two other Shifters who will experience their first full moon at the same time as Hayden. They're both males. We've sent four Guardians to keep watch over them while they face their full moon. We have faith they'll be safe."

While many Shifters served as Dark Guardians, at any one time only twelve sat at the council table, planned strategies, and placed their lives on the line to protect us. Lucas looked over at me. "We believe more will be needed to protect Hayden." He nodded toward his grandfather. "Elder Wilde will explain."

He sat down and Elder Wilde stood. "You were all here when the harvester took Justin. You know what it is capable of."

Elder Thomas's hand tightened on mine, but because the Dark Guardians hadn't heard anything that was not expected, I experienced no spikes in anyone's emotions. As a matter of fact, I was surprised by the calm that pervaded the room. Determination, confidence, even eagerness to confront the enemy slapped at the weak wall I'd managed to somehow erect.

Or perhaps the ferocity of my own emotions made

everyone else's pale in comparison.

"So how do we kick its butt?" Brittany asked.

"You must fight it without shifting," Elder Wilde said. "And for that you need a special weapon. Come with us."

Everyone rose and followed as the elders led us out of the room, along a hallway, down some stairs, and along another hallway to the room where the ancient texts were stored. We were allowed in this room only by invitation. But they didn't stop here. They wended their way among chairs and boxes that housed treasures. They led us around stacks of books and papers. They escorted us to a bookcase.

Elder Thomas reached up and touched a statue of a wolf that rested on one of the shelves. The bookcase swung open.

I could sense everyone's awe. A secret revealed. A hidden place that we'd not known about. We followed the elders into a narrow stone passageway and down another set of stairs to a large wooden door with ornate carvings. Elder Wilde removed a key from his pocket, inserted it into the lock. A click echoed around us. He pushed the door open and led us into a darkened chamber.

Someone flicked a switch and a light illuminated the room.

"Our armory," Elder Wilde said.

I stared in wonder at all the weapons on the walls. Ancient tools of destruction. Swords, knives, axes, clubs—

"Is that Excalibur?" Connor asked.

"These are the weapons that concern you today, young warriors," Elder Wilde said as he indicated a rack of rapiers, ignoring Connor's question.

The handles were gold, but the blades gleamed silver.

"They are made of steel, coated in silver. Just as silver can kill us, it can kill a harvester," Elder Wilde explained. "But this particular weapon has been tempered with magic. It must be embedded in the harvester's heart."

"I can do that," Brittany said, reaching for a sword.

"All of you will need to begin practicing with the swords. Time is short. We will work outside." He looked at me. "Except for you, Hayden. Your shift will occupy you—mind, body, spirit. The Dark Guardians who remain here will accompany you to your transformation, protect you as much as possible. The harvester will attack when your shift begins."

"And then they'll attack it?"

"Yes."

I glanced over at Daniel. If he was my mate, he wouldn't be fighting either—he'd be distracted.

"Still, I want to learn how to fight with a sword," I said. "Anything could happen out there."

In the heat of battle we'd have to be careful not to slice into any Dark Guardians. Our healing properties didn't apply to a wound made by silver.

"So it shall be," Elder Wilde said.

The swords they gave us to practice with were not the ones we'd use during the actual confrontation. Silver was too risky. Wooden swords probably would have been better, only we didn't have any. Besides, we needed to get used to the weight. So steel swords it was.

We went outside, into the yard between the side of the manor and where the forest began some yards away. I didn't think it was coincidence that I was paired with Daniel. I thought the elders were still doing some match-making. Everyone else was matched with their mate, except Seth, who had no mate. I felt for him. He was matched with Elder Thomas.

"The most important thing," Elder Wilde said, "is to become one with the battle, to follow it, to immerse yourself in it. You cannot be distracted. You must concentrate."

I felt everyone's emotions peppering me. Anticipation, excitement, a little anxiety about the possibility of failure. Staying focused during practice was going to be a challenge. I couldn't imagine how I would manage it in the heat of battle.

"Too bad you can't distract me from everyone's feelings now like you did last night," I said to Daniel.

He grinned. "Well, I could but holding you so close doesn't leave much room for wielding our training swords."

I returned his smile. "I don't think you're taking this seriously."

"If I'm your mate, I'll be occupied."

I shook my head. "No, I'm not going to have a mate."

"You can't go through it alone."

"And you've been ordered not to shift."

"You always want to have your weapon out and pointed at your opponent's heart," Elder Wilde said, interrupting my discussion with Daniel—which I considered a good thing.

I knew I was going to have to go through my shift alone. The problem was going to be convincing Daniel. But right now we both needed to learn how to fight.

Elder Wilde gave us a few more tips on stance and balance. Then the yard was echoing with the clash of swords.

I was surprised by the way my arm reverberated with each blow that I parried. We must have practiced for a half hour before the elders told us to take a break. I wasn't wearing a coat. It would hinder my movements. But I wasn't cold. At least not until I stopped moving around.

Daniel came over and put his arm around me, tucking me against his side. "You're pretty good."

I shrugged. "But I won't be the one with a sword. Don't even know why I'm practicing. Just need to feel like I'm doing something."

"You are doing something. You're serving as the bait." I heard in his voice that he didn't like it at all. "I could shift first, draw him out."

"No!" I wrapped my arm around him. "Besides, it's me he really wants. He might just ignore you. Or he could kill you and then come after me. He took out your entire family. He can move quickly, Daniel. Maybe he can even kill two at once. Who knows?"

"I just don't like this plan."

"I trust the elders."

He glanced over to where they were talking.

"I know it's harder for you because you didn't grow up with them," I said, "but they know the best way to handle the ancient dangers."

"With silver swords? Why not a silver bullet? A gun would be better."

I shrugged. "For some reason it has to be a sword. Maybe it's the amount of silver, or the length of it, or who knows? It's an ancient evil and this is what we need to defeat it."

Daniel seemed to contemplate that, and then he called out, "Elder Wilde, will the harvester have a sword?"

"No."

"Then shouldn't we be learning how to bring it down when he'll have a lot more mobility?"

"Indeed, Guardian Foster. That is the next lesson."

The girls and Seth kept the swords while each guy pretended to be a harvester. We were still matched up one-on-one, and my partner was Daniel, who was darting in and out, scrambling around me. I swung, lunged, plunged without actually trying to poke the sword into him. We parried, feinted, jabbed. I swung the sword in an arc. I tried a fancy figure eight to keep him off guard. I worked to keep all the space around me a Daniel-free zone. My arms grew tired. I grew tired.

"You're trying too hard, Hayden," Elder Wilde said as he came up behind me, put his arms around me, and his hands over mine on the sword. "Wait, watch. Strike only once. When the moment is right. But always be ready for that perfect moment."

Daniel lunged and withdrew. He maneuvered around me. He reminded me of a defensive player on a football team trying to get in for the tackle.

We waited, waited, swung—

Daniel leaped back and landed on his butt in the snow.

"We shall claim that as a strike," Elder Wilde said, releasing his hold on me.

"You weren't even close," Daniel said.

Guys and their egos, their need to win.

He scrambled back to his feet.

"Try again, Hayden," Elder Wilde said.

Daniel and I began the process again. I was finding it increasingly difficult to concentrate as the others improved, began taking pride in their accomplishments, began to gain confidence with the weapons. Their feelings bombarded me, made me grow dizzy, confused.

Daniel lunged for me. Not wanting to hit his heart, I brought the weapon around low. I don't know if he moved too slow or I moved too fast, but it sliced into his thigh. Releasing a cry, he reacted without thinking and tried to shove it away, which resulted in him cutting his hand.

He dropped to the ground. The snowy area around him began turning crimson.

THIRTEEN

"Oh. My. God. Daniel." I knelt beside him.

"It's okay," he said, packing snow on his thigh to slow the bleeding.

I barely heard his words as from the others worry, concern, even hints of fear—that it could have been one of them—infiltrated me and surpassed my own fears and worry for Daniel. We had no doctor here.

Reaching out, Daniel took my hand. Still so warm. "Hayden, it's okay. I'll just shift."

"No," Elder Wilde and I said at the same time.

"The risk is too great," Elder Wilde continued.

"This isn't going to heal on its own by tomorrow night," Daniel said.

"Then you will go into battle wounded or not at all. We shall see how you fare tomorrow," Elder Wilde said.

Daniel was shaking his head.

"We do what is best for the pack here, Daniel," Elder Wilde said. "We discussed this when you first came to us. You either adopt our ways or leave."

I watched as Daniel's jaw tightened. I didn't know what he was feeling, but I knew what he was thinking. "Please don't go," I whispered.

He hesitated, then nodded.

"Let's tend to your wounds," Elder Wilde said.

It hurt watching Daniel limp into the manor, leaving a trail spotted with blood in his wake.

"Sucks for Daniel," Brittany said, coming up beside me, "but at least you know you can handle a sword."

"Not that it'll really do you any good tomorrow night," Lindsey said. "You won't have the strength to lift a weapon during your transformation."

Every time I tried to be normal, something happened to remind me that I wasn't.

Inside the kitchen Daniel took a chair.

"I could send for a doctor," Elder Wilde said.

Daniel grimaced. "I'll be fine."

Using scissors, I cut the tear in his jeans so it was larger and we had easier access to his wound. All the emotions . . . I couldn't concentrate.

"I'll tend to Daniel," I said, "but I need everyone to leave except Brittany."

The emotions hammering at me eased slightly, so I could focus on the task. Using warm water, Brittany and I cleaned the wounds and wrapped them in strips of sheet that one of the elders brought us.

"Stop looking so guilty," Daniel said. "It was stupid for us to be practicing against each other. The whole thing is stupid."

I touched his cheek. "You're worried about me."

"Damned right I'm worried. No one has deliberately battled this creature in centuries. What if it's evolved into something that can't be killed with silver? What if . . . There just has to be another way."

I touched his knee. "How bad do you hurt?"

"Bad enough that I'm going to go lie down. Maybe if I rest, the wounds will heal while I sleep."

I watched him struggle to his feet and limp from the room, bandages around his thigh and his hand. I wanted to hit something.

"He's right," I said, but Brittany was there to hear it. "It was stupid."

"It was an accident," she said. "And I disagree. We needed some practice. If we have to take this thing down with a sword, then that's what we have to do."

I sighed. Maybe.

"You know what would make him feel better?" Brittany asked. "Some chocolate cookies."

I stared at her. "How do you know that?"

"When we took that group of girls camping last summer, he ate s'mores like you wouldn't believe. He confessed to me that he's a chocolate addict."

It bothered me that she knew how to comfort him and I didn't.

"What else did he confess?" I asked.

She shook her head and grimaced. "Sorry. I can't really remember. I wasn't paying that much attention. I was determined not to like him. I don't know why I suddenly remembered the chocolate thing. So the cook will be in here before too long to start preparing dinner. Want to get Kayla and Lindsey in here to help us make some cookies before then?"

I thought about passing on the offer, but I did want to do something for Daniel and having only the girls in here would give me more practice at blocking their emotions, or at least let me get used to having them around. My gift was going to be my worst liability tomorrow night.

"Yeah, sure."

I took a quick shower to get Daniel's blood off me and changed into clean jeans and a sweater. On my way back to the kitchen I stopped by the door into Daniel's room. I thought about opening it and just peering in at

166

him sleeping, but I was afraid if I did, I wouldn't return to the kitchen. I'd just want to snuggle against him. I missed that we couldn't seem to find any private moments here.

I put my hand on the doorknob, then shook my head and headed downstairs.

Before I even reached the kitchen, I was swamped with happiness, joy, calm—no doubt all of it coming from the girls in the kitchen. This little afternoon girl time might be just what I needed—whether I could hold back their emotions or not.

When I walked through the door, something soft landed on my face and I heard laughter around me. It was an apron. Did anyone wear aprons anymore? I couldn't recall ever seeing my mom in one.

"We're not exactly the neatest cooks," Kayla said as though she read my mind.

They were already wearing aprons of their own, so I tied mine around my waist, feeling like little Miss Suzy Homemaker. I walked to the huge butcher block. In the center of it were a large blue bowl and a saucepan.

"Okay," Kayla said. "Here is how it works. We're each going to put an ingredient into the saucepan. The person who is putting in the ingredient gets to ask a question and the others have to answer."

"She has to answer, too," Brittany said.

Kayla rolled her eyes. "Maybe. But I'm going first."

And she grabbed the pan before anyone else could.

She dumped in two cups of sugar. "Okay, what are your mate's kisses like?"

Lindsey and Brittany groaned good-naturedly. I was standing there thinking that there might be something worse than feeling someone's emotions: actually describing something as intimate as a kiss.

"Okay," Lindsey said, laughing. "I'll go first, but I'm next with the saucepan."

Her complexion was fair so her blush was visible as it raced into her cheeks. I didn't understand why she would tell us something that embarrassed her, but then I felt trust curling through me, not only hers, I thought, but the others' as well. They trusted one another enough to say anything. They were trying to extend this privilege to me.

"It should come as no surprise that Rafe is an awesome kisser," she said, her blush deepening. "He is so into it that when he's kissing me, I really can't think of anything else."

I thought of last night when Seth's fears were overtaking me. Daniel's kiss had been so powerful that every other emotion except my own receded.

Lindsey looked at Brittany.

Brittany smirked. "You might think you know how Connor kisses but you don't. I guarantee he never kissed you the way he kisses me or you'd have never let him go."

Lindsey smiled. "Aren't you glad I did, though?"

Brittany nodded. "Yeah."

"It wasn't because I didn't think he was terrific, Brit," Lindsey said. "That's the reason I struggled with it so much. Connor's great. He just wasn't right for me."

"She really did struggle with her decision," I said, then felt my own face heat up as three pairs of eyes came to bear on me. "I'm sorry. I don't ever talk about the emotions that visit me—and I didn't know it was you at the time, Lindsey. I just knew there were powerful doubt and guilt being felt by someone. I only figured out that it was you later when things ended up the way they did. And I just—I can feel now—an uncomfortableness. I think it's between you and Brittany. I mean, who else is here, right? I'm sorry. I shouldn't have said anything. I shouldn't be trying to do this bonding cookie thing. I'm just going to go."

I started to turn away, but three *no*s echoed through the kitchen. Brittany was the one who grabbed my arm first, but Kayla was right behind her, taking the other one, and her remorse flowed into me.

"Don't leave," Brittany said. "We can't imagine what it is to be you. To know what everyone's feeling. To hold our secrets."

"Not your secrets. I don't know what you're thinking.

169

I just know what people feel. And the emotions hit me. I don't always know who they're attached to. But sometimes I can figure it out."

"So stay," Kayla said. "We won't do the stupid questions."

"I liked the question," Brittany said. "I wondered what Daniel kissed like. We never kissed. So?"

They released their grips on my arms. I almost ran. Instead I said, "Well, the question was what are your mate's kisses like. And he's not my mate."

"You're not going to accept him?" Brittany asked as they steered me toward the island.

"I don't know."

Lindsey dumped cocoa into the saucepan. "Why not?"

Brittany poured half a cup of milk into the pan before handing it to me along with a stick of margarine. I focused on unwrapping the stick of margarine. It was easier to talk when I wasn't looking at them. "I've never . . . really spent any time with guys. I like him. I like him a lot. He's bossy, but strong and sexy and nice." I dropped the margarine into the pan before looking up. "How did you know your mate was your mate?"

Kayla took the pan to the stove, set the heat on medium, and began stirring the ingredients to melt them. "I didn't even know about mates when I met Lucas," she said, "but wow, something about him really got to me. It was like no matter where he was I could feel him watching me. The depth of attraction I felt for him so fast scared me. I tried to ignore it, pretend it wasn't there, but it was always simmering beneath the surface. As much as he scared me, not being with him scared me more."

"I always loved Connor," Brittany said. "Since I don't have the mate-for-life gene, I'm probably not the best one to explain how you *know* he's your mate."

"But you knew you loved him," Lindsey said.

"Oh yeah. I lived for those moments when I saw him, when he spoke to me, when he just looked at me. I always felt warm and fuzzy if he gave me any attention. He could also piss me off quicker than anyone I knew. When he'd challenge my fighting ability—watch out."

"See, I didn't get that with Connor," Lindsey said. "Being with Connor was . . . pleasant. Enjoyable. Being with Rafe . . . scared the living crap out of me. Still does. Everything is just so intense."

I didn't want to tell them that everything they'd experienced with their mates, I'd experienced with Daniel. It was so personal and private. But was it enough? Why couldn't I just say he was the one?

The mixture began to boil. Kayla removed it from the stove and carried it back to the island, where Brittany dumped three cups of oats, a cup of coconut, and a teaspoon of vanilla into the bowl. "Now the magic ingredient," she said, and added a half teaspoon of imitation butter flavoring.

Kayla poured the chocolate brew into the bowl and Lindsey stirred it. They worked as a team, each seeming to know what the other was going to do. And though they were trying to include me, I still felt slightly like an outsider.

Brittany set a large cookie sheet covered in wax paper on the island and handed me two spoons. Lindsey set the bowl in the center of the island. We began spooning out the concoction and dropping it in little balls on the cookie sheet.

"So what are you going to do about Daniel?" Brittany asked.

"I don't know. It's kind of a moot point, really. I mean, I have to go through my first transformation alone. He can't shift with me."

"That really sucks," Brittany said. "What if you do die?"

"As long as you guys kill that monster . . ." I shrugged, trying to pretend that it didn't matter, that I wasn't scared. I was so glad they couldn't sense my emotions.

I also realized that I'd managed to spend a little time with them without being overwhelmed by theirs.

"So do we bake these or what?" I asked, wanting to

turn the attention away from tomorrow night.

"Nope," Kayla said. "We just let them set." She touched one with the tip of her finger. "Maybe five, ten minutes."

"That's the reason we like them," Lindsey said. "They're easy and quick."

"We should have included you more often," Brittany said quietly.

She'd faced her full moon alone. Although I hadn't been able to feel her emotions, I was certain she'd experienced fear and apprehension. Then disappointment when the moon arrived and left and she remained unchanged. Probably more than anyone, she understood what was going through me.

"Here," she said, taking a small plate and placing some of the cookies on it. "Why don't you take some to Daniel?"

And *maybe have a few minutes alone with him in his room* went unsaid. I felt myself blush again. I didn't think I'd ever blushed so much in my life.

"Thanks," I said, taking the plate. "And thanks for letting me help with the cookies."

"Everything's going to work out tomorrow night," Kayla said.

But I felt her doubts. Sometimes it sucked to be me.

I gave them a brave smile and left the kitchen. Most of

my time with them had been enjoyable. I wouldn't mind hanging out with them again.

I strode through the manor, passing tables of knick-knacks that were hundreds of years old, artifacts of another time. Portraits of generations that had come before lined the wall. The manor was more like a museum than a home.

As I went up the stairs, my heart began pounding and my palms grew sweaty. As much as I was anticipating seeing Daniel, I hated to think of him in pain. But that was preferable to what might happen if he shifted to heal and the harvester became aware of it. We didn't even have aspirin around. A couple of Shifters were pediatricians. They came here during the summer and winter solstice to be on hand if any children got hurt. But once we'd had our full moon, we had no need for their services.

I went down the hallway that led to Daniel's room. I rapped lightly on the door. "Daniel?"

He didn't answer. I wondered if he was in a deep sleep. I didn't think he'd ignore me. He'd said he didn't blame me for what had happened.

I knocked a little louder. "Daniel?"

Again no answer. I pressed my ear to the door. I couldn't hear any movement. What if he'd bled to death? Had the wound been that serious? I didn't think so. But what did I know about wounds?

No, he was probably just sound asleep. Should I disturb him? I didn't have to wake him up. I could leave the cookies on the bedside table for him to find when he woke up.

With my hand trembling in anticipation of seeing him again, I opened the door and peered inside.

His bed was empty. He was gone.

FOURTEEN

I opened myself to allowing in others' emotions. I was searching for the guys. I figured he'd gone to join them, to discuss strategy or fighting or something.

The emotions began roiling through me. Lots of testosterone-type feelings: bravado, challenging. And then they shifted to joy, pleasure, desire. The girls had obviously joined them.

I found them in the game room, which was situated near the media room. But when I walked in, I didn't see Daniel.

"He didn't want the cookies?" Brittany asked.

Her voice forced me through the fog of their emotions.

I hadn't realized they'd noticed me coming in. "He wasn't there."

I felt their alarm spike through me.

"Where'd he go?" Seth asked.

"Well, duh, she wouldn't be here if she knew," Brittany said.

"We need to search for him," Lucas said.

"Or not," I rushed in to say. "Maybe he just wanted to be alone, to nurse his wounds . . ." And even as I said it, I realized that was exactly what he'd gone off to do. Only he'd shift to do it.

"Crap," Lucas said as if the same thought had hit him. "Can you sense if he's in trouble?"

"His emotions don't reach me." Had I never told them that?

"Why not?" Connor asked.

I shook my head. "I don't know."

"Is it something we need to worry about?" Kayla asked.

"No," Lucas said. "Not now. We just need to find him. Fan out; search inside and out."

After they dispersed, I set the plate down on a table and began my own search.

I was pretty certain he wouldn't go outside. Mostly because he had to know that was where we'd search for him. He hadn't shifted in his room, so he'd wanted someplace where he wouldn't be discovered. Maybe someplace with a lock. Maybe even someplace where no one would look.

Always when I'd wanted complete privacy, I'd headed to my reading nook. But Daniel probably wasn't as familiar with the nooks and crannies in the manor.

What he did know was what the elders had revealed to us this afternoon. My heart kicked up its beat. I wasn't certain how I knew where I'd find him. Was this what the girls had been talking about when we'd been making cookies? Was this a sign that he was my true mate?

I followed the path the elders had led us on that morning. When I got to the room where the ancient texts were kept, I walked through to the bookcase and touched the wolf statue. The shelves creaked open. I looked around, spotted a flashlight, grabbed it, and followed the stairs down.

The door to the armory was closed. I tried to open it. Locked. I banged on it. "Daniel!"

I pressed my ear to the heavy wooden door. Thought I heard motion within the room. "Daniel?"

"Just a minute," he fairly growled.

The door opened, barely. I caught a glimpse of him pulling his shirt on. I'd never seen him without clothes, and lately they had been thick winter clothes. He was all lean and muscular. I caught a peek of a stomach so flat and taut that I could have balanced a mug of hot chocolate on it. My mouth went dry.

His head popped up through the opening of his sweater. "What?"

He sounded—and looked—seriously irritated with me.

"You. Shifted."

"So? Did you really think I was going into battle with a gimp leg?"

In retrospect, no.

"Do you know the chance you took? I could have found you in here dead."

"But you didn't. Besides, if the bastard showed, I had a silver sword nearby."

"If it was that easy to kill, it'd be dead by now."

"So what are we arguing about?"

"That you took a chance—"

"A chance that worked, as it turns out." Stepping out, he closed the door behind him. "My leg is as good as new."

"You should have had someone watch over you."

"And I should have been there when my family was killed. Shoulds don't mean anything."

I was never going to win this argument. Besides, why was I mad? He was healed, which increased his chances of surviving tomorrow night. Maybe I was hurt that he hadn't confided in me, that he'd felt the need to be all secretive about it. Maybe I was also disappointed that I'd missed a chance to see him in wolf form—although he'd had to shift back to open the door.

"How'd you unlock the door anyway?"

He held up a key. "I took a criminology class. Do you know burglars can clean out a house in about five minutes, finding all the important stuff because people hide things in obvious places? The elders hid the key right where a criminal mastermind would look."

"So you're a criminal mastermind?"

"Have to think like one to beat one."

"So we have to think like a harvester?"

"I think we already are. We know he's coming for you." He touched my cheek. "I didn't mean to worry you."

"I made you some cookies," I grumbled.

"Awesome."

I started for the stairs. "I'd ask you to promise not to shift again, but since you broke the last one—"

He grabbed my arm and spun me around. "I didn't break the promise. I told you I wouldn't shift unless I had to. I had to. I had to be at my best physically to protect you. I know I haven't officially declared you as my mate in front of the others and that you haven't accepted me, but I think I'm going to be getting that ink on my shoulder soon." He cradled my face. "Don't you understand, Hayden? I'd do anything, take any chance, to protect you."

Then he kissed me, and it terrified me to realize how very much I did understand. Because I'd do anything to protect him.

FIFTEEN

The elders were less than thrilled with the fact that Daniel had shifted. Since his hand was no longer bandaged and he wasn't limping, it was a little difficult to explain the miraculous healing other than with the truth.

As a result, he got stuck washing the dishes after dinner. When he was finished, he joined me in the game room. I was sitting on a stool at the refreshment bar. He sat beside me.

"It'll come tomorrow night," I said softly.

Tension was high. To alleviate some of it, the guys had challenged the girls to a Wii tennis tournament. I was having some success at shielding their emotions, probably because, even though they were engaged in spirited play, there was still a somberness in the air.

"We're going to have a lot of Dark Guardians surrounding you," Daniel said. "The harvester won't be able to get to you."

"And if they die trying to save me? How am I supposed to live with that?"

He took my hand, turned it over, and trailed his finger along my palm where the splinter had been the night we'd played pool. "If you're thinking about doing something stupid like running away again, know that I'll find you."

My heart turned over. I took his hand, brought it to my lips, and kissed it. "I wish we *could* run away."

And wished I'd known him longer. Had gotten to know him better.

"Their emotions are going to ratchet up before the night is over. You're going to take a battering," he said quietly.

"Probably."

He glanced toward those engaged in the tournament, then turned back to me. "When I first came to Wolford, I did some exploring. I found a place. I'd like to share it with you. Tonight. Will you go with me?"

And I knew he was asking just in case one of us didn't survive tomorrow.

I glanced around. The elders would be majorly pissed,

183

but I'd had a taste of absolute freedom—no teachers, no headmistress, no elders—when I'd ventured into Athena. But there was safety with the pack.

Regrettably I shook my head. "You could get hurt or killed."

"No way. I've spent most of my life alone. I fight better alone."

I must have given him a funny look, because he instantly looked as though he'd regretted what he'd said. "But your family—"

"I didn't live with them."

"Ever?"

"The last few years I didn't." He leaned in and whispered, "Want to know the story? Come with me."

It was tempting, so tempting.

"You'll be safe," he insisted. "Until you have the ability to shift—"

"It could try to abduct me."

"It could do that here. Besides, I don't think it has the substance to do that. I mean, it's an ethereal being. It's only solid while it harvests, which is why it's so hard to destroy. There's only a small window of time."

"How do you know so much?"

"Because after Justin was killed and I realized this monster killed my family, I've been researching everything I could find about them. Ask the elders. They'll know."

"And you won't risk shifting?"

"My promise hasn't changed. It's the same as before. I won't shift unless I have to."

"Okay, then," I said. "I'll go with you."

"Are you sure this is wise?" Brittany asked me.

She was sitting on her bed, watching as I packed my backpack. "No."

I wished it was summer so I could wear something that showed a little more of my skin.

"Then why are you doing it?" she asked.

"To be with Daniel. In case tomorrow night . . ." I let my words trail off. No sense in giving voice to my fears.

She wrapped her arms around her legs, drawing them to her chest. "Do you love him?"

I felt my face heat up. "I don't know. I have a hard time understanding my own emotions."

"We all do," she said. "It can get confusing."

I plopped down on the bed and faced her. "How did you know you loved Connor?"

"He was all I thought about. I wanted to be with him—even if it was only to be in the same room."

"But you knew him, because you'd grown up together."

"Yeah. So?"

"I don't know Daniel. My body, my heart reacts to

him, but there is so much that I don't know."

"So you're going to go out in the woods tonight and play Twenty Questions?" She arched a dark brow in a way that said I was kidding myself.

"Maybe Five Questions," I said.

She laughed. "Two. Then you'll be kissing and . . ." She shrugged.

"It just seems that I should know my possible mate before my transformation. It binds you, right?" I grimaced. "Sorry."

She waved her hand. "That's okay. Sometimes I mourn that I'm not a Shifter, but it doesn't seem to make any difference to Connor. He says he fell in love with me the human way, which is slowly and over time, instead of the Shifter way, which too often is simply *bam!*"

"With Daniel it's something in between that. For the first time in my life I *want* to feel someone's emotions and I can't even guess what's he's feeling most of the time."

"And you think tonight . . ."

Might be all I ever had.

Daniel and I headed out after dinner. The moon, a bright silver orb in the night sky, looked so close that I thought I could almost reach out and touch it. The stars were like diamonds spread across velvet. It was such a clear night. The air brisk. Not a hint of wisps, fog, or clouds to mar the brightness.

We didn't take the snowmobile; we hiked. Maybe Daniel worried about alerting the elders to our unsanctioned leaving. But I thought the reason we were walking rested in the camaraderie that came from our trudging along together. We were holding hands, and I realized how much I liked that aspect about him: that he was so comfortable touching, that he seemed always to yearn for it. He never missed an opportunity to touch me.

I'd gone so much of my life not being touched by Shifters. While I'd sometimes embraced girls at school, it wasn't the same. Their history, their world, was so different from mine.

The moon was high in the sky when Daniel finally led me into a cave. It was pitch-black. I felt the chill of the air against my cheeks.

"Wait here," he said quietly.

A click sounded, and the flame from a lighter illuminated his face as he bent and lit a candle. Something magical unfurled around me as I watched him circle the room, lighting the various candles, and the flames began to flicker, slowly revealing the haven he'd created for us.

I knew he must have come here earlier in the day to prepare everything. A mound of blankets formed a pallet on the floor, wide enough that we could sleep separately if that was what I wanted. I knew Daniel wouldn't push for anything tonight. Tonight was just about us growing closer, learning more about each other. Choosing a mate wasn't to be taken lightly. And it certainly wasn't a decision that resided with the elders. I knew they meant well, but in the end a connection had to exist between the two Shifters who were destined to be mates.

I knew I cared about Daniel. Knew he cared about me. But was that enough?

He returned to my side, took my backpack, and carried it to the corner, where he deposited it along with his own. Then he returned to me. "It's not cold once you get used to it."

"When did you arrange all this?" I asked.

"First thing this morning before everyone else was awake."

Taking my hand, he led me into another chamber. I heard the familiar click of the lighter. As he lit the candles, the flickering flames unwrapped his gift to me. An underground pool, with steam rising from it. Stacked neatly along the rocky ledge were towels.

"This is what amazes me," he said, his voice echoing off the cavernous walls. He flicked on a flashlight and shone it in the pool. The water was astonishingly clear. I could see clear down to the rock-covered floor.

"No gunk," he said. "No algae, no crap. It's the kind

of place that health nuts would have used a hundred years ago."

"No critters or creatures?" I asked.

"I've never seen any, and I've been here quite a few times since I discovered it."

"For solitude?" I asked.

"Yeah. I . . . Sometimes I need my space. I love Wolford, I appreciate that everyone has accepted me, but groups aren't really my thing."

I remembered how my impression of him that first day in Athena was that he was a loner. He'd done nothing to dispel that notion, but it seemed more profound when he put the idea into words. Being alone wasn't the way of our kind. Although I'd spent a good deal of my time away from Shifters, there was always that yearning to rejoin them, to belong. It was the reason that I subjected myself to visits every summer and winter. "But being a Shifter is all about being part of the pack."

"Yeah, I know. But it's never been that way for me. Which is why what I feel for you is so special. I've never before wanted to have someone with whom I belonged."

Before I could even think of a response, he flicked off the flashlight, set it aside, came back to my side, and took my hands. Although I still wore my gloves, I could feel that his hands were steady and sure. "I thought you'd like to go swimming," he said tenderly, his voice filling the small cave. "It's almost like a hot tub. In some areas you can feel the water bubbling up from somewhere even farther underground."

I squeezed his hands, tried to look sassy but probably only appeared ridiculous. I'd never anticipated anything so much in my life, and I wanted to do it right. "Are you going to join me?"

I saw the appreciation for my invitation in his eyes. Maybe I hadn't sounded totally silly with my efforts.

"Once you're in the water. Just call for me," he said.

"All right. I can do that."

He brushed his lips over mine. It wasn't enough, but I figured once we were in the pool together, we'd share more. Much, much more.

He left me alone. Removing my gloves, I crouched and skimmed my fingers along the surface of the pool. The water was incredibly warm, almost like a sauna. Hard to believe in the middle of winter, but it was probably coming up through an underground hot spring.

Quickly I removed my clothes and slipped into the pool. It felt wonderful as the silky moisture wrapped around me. I wasn't going to think about tomorrow night. I wasn't going to think about the dangers headed our way or how scared I was when my mind slipped off-task and I thought about the harvester. I was going to make the most of this gift from Daniel. I was going to enjoy it as though my life depended on it. Treading water, I relaxed, allowed the warmth to ease the tension in all my muscles. Then I called out, almost giddy with anticipation, "Daniel!"

I watched as a shadow appeared on the wall near the entryway. Low. Four legs. He was coming to me in animal form. At last I was going to see him as a wolf. My breath backed up in my lungs and I glided over to the lip of the pool.

But what stalked into the small cavern wasn't what I expected. It wasn't a wolf. It was a panther. *The* panther. The one I'd seen in the woods that first night after we left Athena. I was sure of it. But it couldn't be Daniel. That night he'd been back at the camp—

After the panther had sprinted away. Daniel had seemed surprised by my revelation that I'd seen a panther. But if he was the creature, then his response had simply been a ploy to throw me offtrack. "Did it frighten you?" he'd asked. I was beginning to understand why he'd been interested in my reaction then. And I had a feeling he was gauging my reaction now.

The panther was as sleek and beautiful as I remembered. It prowled over to me. Its sinewy muscles undulated with its movements. Its strength and power were evident in each motion. It purred low, a rumble in its throat that echoed around me.

Only when it came to a halt before me and lowered its head did I get a good clear look at its eyes. Green. Like emeralds. And I saw more. So much more.

Because when we shift, everything changes except our eyes. They're the window to our soul. More than our fur, more than the contours of our face, our eyes give us away.

With a tentative hand, dripping with the water from the pool, I reached out and touched its head. "Daniel?"

With a smooth move, like an Olympian scoring a perfect ten, the panther dove into the pool. Daniel emerged from beneath the dark depths.

For several quiet moments, we did nothing except stare at each other, our breaths echoing around us. I didn't know what to say. In a way I felt betrayed that he'd held this secret for so long. This was huge. All along I'd viewed him as one of us, had expected when I did finally see him transform, he would be all that I was accustomed to: thick fur, barks, and canine growls. I knew there were different clans of Shifters, that not all of them transformed into wolves—but I'd never seen members of one. For me they were as much a legend as the harvester had been.

"I thought you should know," he finally said in a low voice. "Before you decide whether or not to accept me as your mate."

Then, because I remained silent, I guess he felt

compelled to add, "I'm not a wolf."

I nodded, blinked, knowing that my first words were crucial, but I wasn't sure what to say, and what I did eventually say was a disappointment even to me when it echoed around us. "Yeah, I just figured that out."

"It bothers you."

"No, I . . . I just wasn't expecting it. It was you rubbing your shoulder against that tree that night in the woods."

"Yeah, I had an itch."

"Why didn't you tell me then?"

"Because you'd told me earlier—again—that you wouldn't accept me as your mate. I figured knowing I wasn't exactly the same breed as you wouldn't earn me any points. I—" He looked up as though he was struggling to find the right words. Then he lowered his gaze back to me. "I told you that I volunteered to find you. The first time I ever saw you, I was intrigued. Yes, the elders selected me to be your mate but only because I stepped forward before anyone else could."

Tears stung my eyes. I'd never felt such a loss for words.

"I know you didn't feel the same when you first saw me," he said. "I thought if you came to know me, to see what we had in common, that what was different about us wouldn't matter."

I was overwhelmed to think he had put so much thought into this, that he had wanted me that much. I thought of all the times he'd touched me, reached out to me.

I shook my head emphatically. "It doesn't matter. That you shift into a panther. I think you're gorgeous."

I couldn't be certain, but I thought he blushed.

"Is that why I can't feel your emotions? Because you're a different breed?" I asked.

"I don't know. I guess."

I'd known something was different about him, but I'd have never guessed this.

"Who knows?" I asked. "That you're not a wolf?"

"No one, as far as I know. The elders may suspect, but they've never said anything. I've worked really hard not to let anyone see me shift."

"Why? Why did you keep it secret from everyone?"

"We're not like you." Shaking his head, he leaned back, stretching out his arms and gripping the sides of the pool. "We don't live in packs. We don't mate for life. Wolves come together and fight for each other. We take on the characteristics of our species. Black panthers, leopards—whatever name you give us—we're loners. We don't seek each other out. Coming here was against my nature."

"Why did you stay, then?"

Leaning his head back, he again studied the rock

194

ceiling as if it held the answer. When he returned his gaze to mine, I couldn't have looked away if I wanted.

"Because we're so solitary, there are only about a dozen of us left. But you won't find us on any endangered species list. I thought if I came here, if I watched the way the wolves worked together, that I'd learn a way to bring my own kind together, to find a way to ensure that as a breed of Shifter we survive."

I gave him a crooked grin. "And instead you almost found yourself with a wolf for a mate."

"I don't want it to be *almost*, Hayden. I want it to happen."

Tears stung my eyes. "It can't. Don't you understand that? If there wasn't a harvester—" What was worse? To know that if there was no harvester, I'd accept him in a heartbeat or to think that I wouldn't accept him under any circumstances? I wanted to be with him so badly. But the timing sucked.

"I'm not afraid of what might happen tomorrow night," he said.

"Well, I am. And you're a fool if you're not."

"Which is why you need a mate. To be there with you. Completely. I think you're the most amazing person I've ever met. If you accept me as your mate, I promise that I'll follow the tradition of your kind and be loyal to you."

195

"Daniel, I can't decide this now," I muttered. He cared enough for me to risk his life, and I cared enough for him not to let him do it.

"Are you . . . appalled by what I am?" he asked.

I almost came up out of the pool. "God, no. Why would you think that?"

"I'm not exactly what you're used to."

"And you've met a lot of girls who experience others' emotions?"

He grinned. "No. I can honestly say that I've never met anyone like you."

And I thought he was talking about more than this ability I possessed, that in an offhanded way he was giving me a compliment. He was baring so much of himself to me. It was what I'd always wanted from a guy. I didn't expect it to be this hard. Because if I gave him reason to think we could be together, if I encouraged him, then tomorrow I could lose him. Was it better to lose him tonight? To reject his heartfelt declarations?

Maybe. But not at that moment. Not yet. I wanted more time with him. But not here.

"I think I'm starting to shrivel," I said. "Can we get out now?"

"Sure. I'll go first and wait for you in the other part of the cave." He started to submerge.

"Daniel?"

Stopping, he looked at me.

I swallowed hard. "It doesn't make any difference to me. What you shift into. Well"—I rolled my eyes—"I'd probably be weirded out if you shifted into a rat or something, but I like you . . . a lot. A whole lot."

"Even though I dragged you back to a place where you didn't want to be?"

Before I could respond, he went beneath the water and emerged from the pool in panther form. In spite of the fact that we had to tear off our clothes in order to shift, we were modest. I watched as his long, sleek body practically stalked out of the cave. He really was gorgeous. Whether he was in panther or human form.

But I didn't know how the bonding worked between different species. I couldn't tap into his emotions. Would he be able to read my thoughts? Would we be able to communicate telepathically when we were in animal form? When we weren't, would we know each other's thoughts like other bonded couples?

Everything he'd told me should have made what I was going to face tomorrow easier. Instead it only made it that much more difficult. Now I had so much more to lose.

"So what does it mean exactly?"

I was lying on the mound of blankets, trailing my finger over Daniel's tattoo. It looked like black fire outlined in brilliant blue bursting out of his shoulder, flames trailing down his bicep. But over the back of his shoulder was a series of Celtic knots. I didn't think they represented my name. I thought he'd respect my wishes enough not to get the symbol for my name tattooed on his shoulder. Besides, this was his right shoulder and the tattoo associated with one's mate usually went on the left, closer to the heart.

Propped up on his elbow, he was stretched out beside me. After I'd left the pool and gotten dressed, I'd joined him. He'd been wearing his shirt until I asked him to take it off. I'd wanted to see his ink, to learn everything about him.

"The different tentacles represent the separation of my kind," he told me now. "Each standing alone. The knots represent your kind—the way they're woven together. They're stronger."

"Wow. You gave it a lot of thought."

"Don't you think we should—to anything that's going to be permanent?"

I knew he was talking about mates. About how the bonding ritual shouldn't be taken lightly. I could honestly say that both of us were giving it a great deal of thought.

"I wish we had more time to be together, to explore our feelings," he said quietly.

I'd always heard that cats were aloof creatures, but I

thought Daniel was searching for a connection, wanted one as badly as I did.

"Before my full moon?" I asked.

"Yeah."

But I wasn't convinced it'd make any difference. I knew how I felt about him. I was falling for him. That wasn't going to change.

"If you're hurt, do you still heal more rapidly in Shifter form?" I asked, thinking how dangerous tomorrow night would be. No matter how much I tried not to let it into my thoughts, it was slithering through anyway. When it did, despair would hit me and I'd fight it back. I didn't want anything to ruin this moment.

"Yes. I'm like you in every way except I turn into a panther. Oh, and I don't feel others' emotions."

"So you can read the other Shifters' thoughts when you're in panther form?"

"Yeah. That's a common connection between us, I guess."

"Can you read my thoughts now?"

Disappointment flashed in his eyes. He knew where I was going with this. "No."

"They say true mates know what the other is thinking, even when they're in human form."

"Maybe it happens after the bond is created with the first shift."

"Maybe. So how did you . . . I mean, if your kind doesn't hang out together, how did you learn about your family?"

"Came home from my first year at college—found them. My family was close, but I couldn't tell you where any other Shifters in the area lived. We didn't seek each other out. My mom had mentioned Wolford, talked about other clans of Shifters. She knew a little of the history. Enough to get me here."

I skimmed my fingers up into his hair. "I can't imagine what you must have felt. Finding them."

Taking my hand, he nibbled on my fingers, signaling that he was changing the subject, that he didn't want to take a trip down Memory Lane into the dark memories. "I don't want anything to happen to you when you face your full moon."

I forced myself to grin. "Well, something's going to happen. I'll transform."

"Are you afraid?"

I was, for myself and him, but I wasn't going to admit it to him, so I shook my head. "Not yet anyway. Who knows what I'll feel when the moment comes."

Threading his fingers through my hair, he combed them down its length. "I think you're courageous. I don't think it'll defeat you."

"Courageous? Uh, did you forget I ran away?"

He held my gaze. "That took courage. You didn't know what you'd find out there."

Neither had he when he'd begun his trek to Wolford.

"Are we what you thought we'd be?" I asked.

"Better. Everyone welcomed me. I wasn't expecting that."

"Why didn't you let anyone know you're a panther?"

"It's a part of myself I'm not used to sharing. Always hid it from the Statics. Other than my family, no other Shifters were around to share it with. I wasn't ashamed. Just cautious. Didn't know how . . . it would all work out. And I certainly wasn't expecting you. You're strong, Hayden. And that makes you sexy as hell."

Then he kissed me. I loved the way he kissed. Boldly and with confidence. I rolled into him and he tucked me beneath him. His skin was warm beneath my fingers. I loved the strength I felt in his muscles. Even in human form I could feel the lingering remnants of the big cat: sleek, powerful.

I felt safe with him. But I was also afraid. Afraid I'd lose this.

I tried not to think about it. I tried to focus on us, on what I wanted for the future. I fought to remain positive.

We kissed, talked, and laughed throughout the night. Sharing our pasts, what we remembered of our families, our dreams for the future. I thought I should have been tired when the candles burned out and the sunlight crept in through the cave entrance. But I felt rejuvenated, refreshed, ready to face whatever the coming night might bring.

I was prepared to meet my destiny.

And I knew what my answer would be when Daniel declared me as his mate. It would be no. Because I wouldn't risk losing him.

SIXTEEN

We took our time walking back to the manor. It was such a clear, crisp day that it was difficult to accept that a virtual storm was brewing for tonight.

The closer we got to our destination, the more emotions began flittering in and out of me. Anxiety, fear, dread, anticipation. None of them were mine, but they mirrored mine. I wanted to be brave, I wanted to be strong, but the truth was that I was scared. And I resented like hell that the harvester was tainting what should have been an awesome night of awakening and deepening a bond with my mate. When I'd returned to Wolford at the beginning of winter break, I'd been cautiously hopeful that maybe I would find someone willing to go through my first shift with me. But I'd never expected to find someone like Daniel, someone whom I truly wanted to share that moment with. At times what I felt for him seemed too big to contain. And to know that he had such strong feelings for me—it was a gift I'd never truly expected to receive.

I didn't want to throw it back in his face. But I wasn't willing to risk the consequences that came with accepting it. That saddened and infuriated me. I didn't realize how hard I was squeezing Daniel's hand until he joked, "If you don't loosen your grip, I'm going to have to shift to mend a broken bone."

Immediately I let go. "Oh God, I'm sorry."

He gave me a tender smile. "It's okay. Their emotions are starting to invade you, aren't they?"

They were, but they weren't the source of my rising tension or fear. Still I nodded. I wanted to lessen his worries about me.

He calmly glanced around, as though measuring threats and contemplating possibilities. I wondered if anything unsettled him. Now that I knew he was a panther at heart, I understood the stillness that I'd witnessed in him so many times. I could envision him stretched out on a tree branch, his tail swinging lazily.

"Maybe we shouldn't go back," he said. "Maybe we should return to the cave and wait for your full moon.

You don't need to be bombarded all day with everyone else's fears and anxieties. You probably have enough of your own."

More than enough. They not only centered around me but around him. I'd never understood how much responsibility came with love. As incredible as it was to experience the emotion, it was equally terrifying.

His idea was so appealing, to simply spend the rest of the day with him, but I found myself shaking my head. "Maybe while continuing to scour through the ancient texts the elders will have discovered something else to help us." I knew they wanted to find something more foolproof. "I should have stayed with them, helped them search."

He touched my cheek in a familiar gesture that I was coming to expect. He was so tough on the outside, but he held such tenderness. "Do you regret spending last night with me?"

I smiled softly, filtering through the hoarded memories. "I wouldn't trade anything for last night. But now I have to face reality, and that means shoring up walls."

"It sucks."

I laughed. "Yeah, but I'm getting used to it."

"I guess I could distract you with a kiss."

And before I could respond, he did. It was amazing how everything else faded into the background. He was such a great kisser. There was a purpose to the movement of his mouth, almost as though he were painting passion. I didn't want it to stop. But eventually we had to come up for air, and when we did, he pressed his forehead to mine, and said, "Let's go back to the cave."

Oh, it was tempting. So tempting. "Tomorrow."

Leaning back, he studied me, maybe trying to determine if I really thought there would be a tomorrow for us. Finally he accepted whatever it was he saw in my face, took my hand, and started walking back to the manor.

"So have you tried to block the emotions?" he asked.

"Every chance I get. Sometimes it's like there's a shimmering wall there, but I just can't make it materialize into something solid."

"When was the last time you tried?"

I peered over at him. The sight of him always gave my heart a little kick. "What difference does it make?"

He shrugged. "Maybe none. But you're on the cusp of your full moon. Your other senses are heightening. Maybe you'll gain the ability to block out what you don't want to experience."

"That would be sweet." If I could find a way to control what I allowed in, maybe I could even learn to use my ability for something good. "Why do you think your kind scattered?" I asked, needing, wanting to change the subject.

"It's the nature of a panther."

"You mentioned that you'd come here to learn from us, so you could gather your kind back together. Had you planned to stay?"

"Plans change."

Yeah, they did, I thought. Sometimes the unexpected happened. Daniel had been unexpected—in so many ways.

It was still early when we arrived at the manor and went inside. No one was around. Daniel and I went up the stairs. At the landing we turned toward a hallway.

Suddenly emotions flared. Love, desire, so powerful, so strong that they nearly knocked me off my feet. I didn't know who they belonged to, but they humbled me with their intensity. Closing my eyes tightly, I backed against the wall.

"Hayden?"

I shook my head. I had to concentrate. While I knew he could distract me, probably make what I was feeling go away, I wanted to understand what was roiling through me. This was the worst sort of invasion: to know the depths of someone else's feelings. But at the same time love was the one emotion we all craved. This love was so sweet, so pure. It was the type that inspired poets— a thought that would have caused me to gag if I hadn't experienced it and understood the true rarity of it.

Footsteps sounded. Opening my eyes, I fought to push the emotions back, to look unaffected, as the couple rounded the corner.

Brittany and Connor.

I was stunned to realize that the emotions I'd felt were all his, because hers never reached out to me. Did she have any idea how deeply he loved her?

"Hey," Brittany said, smiling warmly. "We were just headed to breakfast. Want to join us?"

"No, thanks. I'm going to shower."

She shrugged. "Okay."

"We're having another practice session in about an hour," Connor said. "You'll both need to be there."

"We'll be there," Daniel responded.

Connor slapped him on the back as he and Brittany walked by.

"What were you feeling from them?" Daniel asked when they were gone.

I winked at him. "I never experience and tell."

The Guardians were already well versed in several combat techniques, so in the courtyard they weren't being taught anything. They were mostly just wrestling around, warming up for tonight's main event when they wouldn't be able to shift. Their primary purpose in being out here was to provide a catalyst for *my* lesson.

While they haphazardly tossed each other around, I sat with my back against a tree and focused on building a wall between their emotions and mine. I would be distracted enough tonight. Closing my eyes, I breathed deeply. Worry slammed into me. Fondness. Anger. Excitement. Anticipation. Affection. Devotion. A kaleidoscope of sentiments. Some stronger than others. Some would fade out while others burst forth. I lost sight of which were mine, and that was what I had to work hard to prevent.

Tonight, with everyone surrounding me, striving to protect me, I couldn't allow their feelings to overwhelm me.

I heard grunts, groans, shouts, and laughter. These Shifters were all connected, by what they were. The elite of our kind. The Dark Guardians. They had a mission, a purpose. I was awed by their sense of camaraderie. I didn't want to push it out. I wanted to be absorbed by it.

I would have let it overtake me completely if I could have controlled what I allowed in. Instead I pushed it back as well. I focused on my own feelings.

Fear. Of tonight and what might happen.

Excitement. Facing an unknown challenge.

Anticipation. Of my first shift.

Concern. That others might be hurt or die because of me.

Affection. For Daniel. So deep, so profound that I knew it was the beginning of love. The feeling was scary and wonderful. But I didn't know what to do with it. I was so focused on it, on trying to figure it out, that it took me a minute to realize that I now was feeling only my own emotions. I could still hear activity nearby.

Slowly, so slowly, I opened my eyes. The others were there, prancing around, avoiding blows, rolling around, jumping to their feet. But their emotions seemed distant, hovering just beyond my reach. Excitement from someone shot through me, and I squelched it. It was difficult and wearisome to hold the emotions at bay. But I realized I could do it. I would do it.

I turned my attention to Daniel. He was so lithe and graceful. I could see the feline in him. How could anyone look at him and not see that he would shift into a great big cat?

He must have felt my gaze on him, because he looked at me. Our eyes met. His green to my caramel. Something sizzled between us. Something powerful. I thought tonight, after my shift, he would be the first thing I'd want to scent.

But I distracted him. Rafe took him down, plowed into him, and buried him in the snow.

My concern for him caused my emotional wall to crumble. All their emotions came rushing in, pounding at me. It took so much to push them back, so little distraction to lose the foothold I'd gained. Daniel was a distraction to me, but worse than that, I was one to him. At a crucial moment would he be more worried about my safety than his? I knew the answer, because mine would be the same. I'd put him first and he'd do the same for me. And it could cost him his life. I had to find a way to ensure he wasn't with me tonight. As badly as I wanted him to be there for the strength I drew from him, I couldn't risk something happening to him. It would kill me as effectively as the harvester's attack.

"Okay!" Lucas shouted. "Let's go inside and do some planning." He slid his arm around Kayla, and I experienced a sense of love that almost took my breath.

As the others began heading inside, Daniel strolled over, his long legs eating up the distance between us. He crouched in front of me, touched my cheek. "For a while there it looked like you were sleeping."

I shook my head. "No. For a little while I could block out their emotions."

His eyes widened and he grinned, sharing my triumph. "Really?"

I smiled back. "Yeah. It was . . . Well, it made me think with more work, I could get better at blocking and unblocking at will."

"You think you'd ever *want* to feel their emotions?"

"I don't know. Under the right circumstances it might prove to be useful."

He straightened and held his hand out to me. I put mine in his, and he pulled me to my feet. As we walked into the manor, I glanced over my shoulder. I could sense the danger lurking, the harvester watching. My heart sped up and a shiver of dread went through me. I pushed back my fears, just as I was learning to push back others' emotions.

But in the end my fears were too strong. They wouldn't be quelled.

"You know, it's really not fair that your first shift is overshadowed by this creature," Kayla said as she brushed my hair.

We were getting together for what I hoped wouldn't be anyone's last meal. Kayla, Lindsey, and Brittany had invited me to get ready with them.

"It should be a night you'll always remember," Lindsey said.

"I think it'll be that," I said as I took the brush from Kayla. I pulled my sandy blond hair back, twisted it up, and clipped it in place.

"My first shift happened at the waterfall," Kayla told us.

"Mine, too," Lindsey said.

The waterfall was in a beautiful area in the forest that we shared with no one. Even in winter it was gorgeous because much of it solidified into ice. It looked like an elaborate sculpture. But the elders didn't want us to travel far.

"Connor took me there after my non-full moon," Brittany said as she leaned into the mirror on the dresser and applied mascara. "We made it special." She slid her gaze over to me. "The special night with your mate can happen anytime. Doesn't *have* to be during your first full moon."

"She's right," Lindsey said. "You can have lots of special moons. Still I think it sucks about tonight."

"Maybe it won't show," Kayla mused. "When it sees how many of us there are and that we have silver swords—"

"It's an evil beast. It has no common sense," Brittany told her.

"Okay, enough talk about the bad," Lindsey said. "Let's talk guys. So you and Daniel . . ." She wiggled her eyebrows. "What happened when you snuck off last night?"

I felt myself blush, sensed their true interest. "We just talked."

"Did he show you his fur?"

Swallowing hard, I nodded. "Yeah."

"So you finally saw him shift!" Brittany said. "Is he gorgeous?"

My face grew hot. I was used to the intimacy of feeling emotions in others but not discussing intimate things. "Uh, yeah."

"All black with those beautiful green eyes—I bet he was stunning."

"Brittany has always cared about appearance," Lindsey scoffed, releasing a little laugh. "I think the way he makes you feel is way more important."

Her gaze homed in on me as though she could bring my most personal thoughts to the surface.

"Guys," Kayla said, "Hayden has only gotten to know us in the past couple of days. We can't expect her to share her most private feelings with us."

We moved on to talking about other things. Clothes and school. I recognized that they were trying to prevent me from thinking about tonight. But it was never far from my mind.

As much as I liked hanging out with the girls, I had to admit that I felt a small sense of relief when we walked into the parlor and I saw Daniel. It was strange—the way my attention zeroed in on him so quickly, as if I instinctively knew where he was.

The guys had exchanged their sweats and T-shirts for

jeans and sweaters. Daniel's were black. I wondered why he'd want to wear any other color when black brought out the brilliance of his eyes. At that moment they were glittering, and I didn't know if it was from the joy of seeing me or from excitement about the upcoming battle.

As Kayla, Lindsey, and Brittany each migrated toward their mates, I felt a little sorry for Seth, who seemed so alone. As far as I knew, he'd never declared a mate. But then, technically, neither had Daniel.

Daniel strolled over to me. "A couple of hours before we head out."

I nodded. "I'm trying not to think about it."

"Hard to shut it off." He glanced over his shoulder. "Are they having any luck doing it?"

I shook my head. "No. But everyone's trying to keep their emotions even, so they don't infringe on my space."

"They care about you," he said. "I don't know if you can feel that."

"I never know who the emotions are directed at. Sometimes I can guess. . . ." I shrugged.

"Don't even think it," he said.

I jerked my gaze back to his, which was smoldering with passion, but I thought it was ignited by anger as well.

"What?" I asked.

"Don't think about going off on your own. You know

I'll find you. They can find you as well."

"Yeah, that whole scent thing is irritating." I narrowed my eyes at him. "So why did it take you so long to find me before, at the ski resort? I was there for a couple of weeks before you showed up."

He grinned that devilish smile. "You were there for a couple of weeks before I let you know I was there."

"So when you said you'd just arrived that day—you lied?"

He shrugged. "I figured it would make you less mad than knowing that I'd been watching you for a while."

"Why wait?"

"You looked happy. You weren't peering out of a window looking sad."

"I don't know if I'm going to stay here, Daniel. After tonight. It's draining, holding their emotions back."

"For what it's worth, I don't know if I'll stay either." He touched my cheek. "We can talk about it later."

We went into the dining room and took our places at the long table. Elder Wilde sat at the head, one elder on each side of him, with Lucas at the foot of the table. I supposed there would come a time when he would take his place at the head of the table but not yet.

I sat between Daniel and Seth. I could sense Seth's nervousness even before I realized that his right leg was constantly in motion, moving up and down, quick jerks.

He'd encountered the harvester before.

I leaned over and whispered, "You don't have to go."

He snapped his head around to look at me, a question in his eyes.

"Tonight," I answered to his unspoken question. "You could stay behind."

I saw a flash of anger, felt it. "I'm not a coward."

"I didn't mean—"

"I'm antsy, that's all. Ready to get started."

"She didn't mean anything, dude," Daniel said, and while I couldn't feel his emotions, I sensed the tenseness in his body.

I didn't want a fight here.

"Sorry," I whispered.

The cook brought out the food. Steak. Rare. Basking in its own red juices. I thought about sticking with my vegetarian diet, but for some reason tonight I craved red meat. *The nearness of my full moon*, I thought. *You can't deny your wolf instincts.*

And wolves are carnivores. Aware of Daniel watching me, I sliced off some meat and ate it. The succulent flavor burst through my mouth. Never had anything tasted so good.

"Heightened taste," he leaned in and whispered, and I could smell the piney scent of him, stronger than before.

"I may never be a vegetarian again." My senses were

becoming stronger. Soon, very soon, the moon would be calling to me.

When we finished eating, we gathered again in the parlor. The elders were standing near the fire. The rest of us were scattered throughout the room, but near enough to hear them easily. I decided all of our nerves were jangling. None of us could sit still.

Fear and anxiety darted in and out of me—but they were mine.

"We will not be going with you," Elder Wilde said, drawing me close, giving me a comforting hug. "We must remain here. The Dark Guardians will protect you."

"I could go alone, with a sword—"

"You will not be able to hold on to it once your shift begins," he pointed out.

"I could try."

"And if you fail, you die."

"But why should they risk their lives for me?"

"Because you are part of the pack."

And I realized there was a price to pay for belonging.

"The girls will help you prepare," he said.

I knew there were rituals, a white robe to be worn. Usually the girl was alone with her mate, and she prepared herself. Nothing for me was the way it was supposed to be.

"Are you ready to face your destiny?" Elder Wilde asked me.

I nodded, my mouth dry, my stomach knotting up.

He gave me a warm smile. "All will be well."

And I wondered if he could see the future or had a crystal ball. I almost mouthed off about it, but out of respect—and because I was more nervous than I'd ever been in my life—I didn't say anything.

"Is there any other business before we adjourn so Hayden may begin the rituals?" Elder Wilde asked.

"Yes, sir," Daniel said, and my heart lurched. He crossed over to me, each stride long and graceful, each movement reminding me of what he was. He moved with the sinewy grace of a predatory cat.

When he reached me, he stopped and held my gaze. "I told you that the elders had asked for someone to step forward and be your mate—and I volunteered—but the final choice is still yours." Holding both my hands in his, he went down on one knee. "I declare you my mate. Hayden, will you accept me?"

Joy and pain riffled through me. I could give him only one answer, and it broke my heart to do it. But I wouldn't risk the one person I loved above all others.

My voice was quiet, sure, and steady. "No."

SEVENTEEN

It was the hardest thing I'd ever done. To say that single word.

I couldn't feel his emotions, but I saw the shock and confusion in his eyes as he slowly straightened. Almost worse was experiencing what everyone else was feeling: disbelief, pity—no doubt for Daniel—sorrow.

I watched as he straightened his shoulders, was keenly aware that he was struggling to hold on to his pride. Knew he would never forgive me for this moment of shame and embarrassment.

And I'd only just begun.

"Daniel isn't one of us," I told Elder Wilde.

I actually felt betrayal ripple through Daniel—or maybe I was just processing the stiffness of his body.

"He shifts into a panther."

More disbelief coming from the others. I heard quiet murmurings. We all knew that not all Shifters were wolves, but I suspected that, like me, none of them had ever known any other kind.

"Have you seen him shift?" Elder Wilde asked.

"Yes. I also know that sometimes when the harvester attacked, Daniel wasn't nearby. I think . . . I think somehow he and the harvester are connected."

"Why in the hell would you think that?" Daniel asked.

I turned to face him. "You told me it killed your parents. You led it here."

He shook his head in denial. "No."

"You know you did! The full moon, the night I ran away. That was the first harvester attack here. It had never found us before that. It started with you, Daniel. It started with you." I looked back at the elder, pleading. "I don't want him with me tonight."

"You can't stop me! You can't—"

Elder Thomas struck so fast that I barely saw it. His hand chopped against Daniel's neck. Daniel dropped to his knees, clearly stunned.

"Lucas, Rafe," Elder Wilde said. "Lock him in the

dungeon. We will deal with this matter later. The time is nearing for Hayden's full moon."

"Are you sure—" Lucas began.

"I'm sure."

They each grabbed his arms. Daniel looked at me with loathing. It blasted into me, and even though I wasn't absorbing the emotion, it still caused a sharp pain in my heart, a pain I was surprised I was able to survive.

As I watched them drag him away, I realized nothing else I faced tonight would be as horrible as what I'd seen in his eyes.

EIGHTEEN

My heart heavy, I trudged through the forest wearing snow boots and a thick, white, velvety robe that I could easily discard once my shift started.

I knew that I'd lost Daniel forever, that he'd never forgive me for turning him away, for making the others doubt him. But if I'd accepted him as my mate, tradition would have dictated that he be beside me now, in a black robe. And during my transformation, he would shift and join me—me in wolf form, he in panther.

And the harvester would have destroyed us both.

I wasn't sure why the first shift couldn't take place within the gates that surrounded the manor. Maybe it had something to do with whatever protected Wolford from the outside world.

Within the forest were special areas—romantic places—that the guys took their mates for their first shift. But we stopped at the first clearing we reached. There would be nothing romantic about tonight.

Kayla laid a quilt over the snow.

"I've never given any thought to what the Shifters who first transform in winter go through," Lindsey said. "Glad my birthday is in summer."

"No kidding," Rafe said. "You'd have gone through it alone."

She slapped playfully at his arm, but there was a nervousness to their energy.

With the exception of Brittany, the Dark Guardians had always battled in wolf form. Now the scabbards were at their sides. They should have looked out of place in this modern world, but on them the swords simply reinforced their destiny as Dark Guardians, warriors who would do whatever they needed to protect our kind.

Tonight the seven of them were there to protect me.

I looked up at the black sky and thought it had never been more beautiful, or more foreboding. The moon was a bright orb, its light filtering through the clouds in front of it, giving them an eerie glow. The stars were vast. I knew the constellations, but for some reason I couldn't make out any of them. Maybe I was as distracted and nervous as the others.

I was pleased with the success I was having at blocking back their emotions, but I knew I would lose this fine tether hold once the battle began. The courage, bravado, fears would surge to heart-pounding levels. I wouldn't be able to ward them off.

All I could do was focus on my own feelings and hope I could somehow remain lucid and able to react to whatever happened.

As though understanding the direction of my thoughts, Kayla put her arms around me. "It's going to be okay."

"Maybe we should have done this in the basement instead," Brittany said.

My stomach knotted up with the thought of Daniel locked there now—and what he must be feeling.

"Good move, Brit," Lindsey said.

"Oh, crap. I'm sorry."

"Brick walls and locks won't keep this creature out," Connor said as he put his arm around her. "No harm, no foul in mentioning Daniel. He's not far from any of our thoughts. How did we not figure him out?"

"Especially me," Brittany said. "I spent the most time with him."

"Yeah, but you were probably ignoring him mostly," Rafe said. "You didn't want him for a mate."

Brittany looked at me. "Not because I didn't think he was cute or anything. And he was nice."

"He just wasn't Connor," I said, forcing a crooked smile.

She snuggled up against her mate. "Yeah."

"Okay," Lucas said. "We need to start preparing."

I looked at the sky. The moon was higher. As soon as it reached its zenith . . .

Removing my fur-lined boots, I tossed them off to the side and stepped onto the quilt. I could still feel the cold easing through to the soles of my feet. I drew the robe more tightly around me. Kayla had brushed my hair to a sheen and tucked a violet bloom near my temple—as though I cared what I looked like.

I wasn't preparing myself to share my first shifting with my mate. I was preparing to face the harbinger of death.

The Dark Guardians circled me.

"Remember," Lucas said to the others, "no matter what your instincts scream at you—do not shift."

The metal rasps of swords leaving scabbards echoed through the night.

"And remember not to stab these things in each other," Connor said.

I knelt on the quilt, hoping I wouldn't become a sacrificial lamb. Turning my face upward, I felt the moonlight caress my skin and thought of Daniel. The boldness with which he'd walked through the door of the chocolate café. The tenderness with which he held me. The heat of his

226

kisses. The beauty of his animal form. Even if I survived tonight, I'd never experience all the myriad wonders of him again.

I felt the first tingle of skin, muscles, bone. As though a gentle current of electricity was flowing through them.

"I think"—I heard the panic in my voice, breathed deeply, calmed myself—"it's starting."

Around me the others adjusted their stances, raised their swords slightly. Seth knelt in front of me on the quilt and laid his sword between us.

Panic rattled through me. "What are you doing?"

"I'm going to guide you through your transformation."

I shook my head emphatically, and my voice was fierce. "No. You can't do that. You can't risk—"

"You'll die—"

"I'll take that chance. I'm not willing to risk someone else. Why do you think I told all those lies about Daniel?"

His eyes widened. "He's not a panther?"

"He is." Tears stung my eyes. "But he's not associated with the harvester. He's the most noble—" My throat clogged. "Please. Please, don't do this."

He looked up at Lucas. I twisted around and faced Lucas, too. "Please," I rasped. "I can do this by myself. But if I'm worried about Seth . . . I have to be able to concentrate."

He hesitated, swore harshly beneath his breath. "Just flow with it. When the pain gets too great. Just flow with it."

I nodded, all the gratitude I felt for his decision reflected in my eyes.

"Seth, get into position," Lucas ordered.

I knew Seth wouldn't have appreciated knowing that I felt immense relief flowing through him. He could bravely face the harvester with sword in hand, but helping me through my transformation had not been his first choice regarding how he wanted to spend tonight. But still I was grateful to him as well. I had always known that the Dark Guardians were the protectors of our kind, but I'd never fully understood the sacrificial lengths they'd go to in order to shield us from harm. I didn't know if I was worthy to be one of them, but I was certainly going to give it my best.

I felt my body tingling, little pinpricks of pain jumping through it as though circuits were being tested.

I was aware of the Guardians taking their positions. I could feel their readiness, their alertness.

But nothing could prepare us for what came up through the ground in front of us.

The harvester had arrived, and he'd brought with him six hounds from hell.

NINETEEN

The Dark Guardians closed their circle around me. The hounds bared their teeth, red saliva dripping from the sharp points. They crouched low, circling around us. I was on all fours, breathing heavily. I could feel the shift coming. My blood was rushing between my ears.

The harvester patiently waited. It was a hideous creature, at least seven feet tall. And broad. Although it wasn't yet fully formed. It was like a mist. Form but no substance. I knew it would become solid when the time came. Those long, taloned fingers would reach out to me, would touch me, would suck out my soul.

Its snarling minions, however, were another story.

They were solid masses, their red eyes gleaming.

Pain shot through me. I released a tiny cry. Kayla was the first to lose her concentration. No surprise. She hadn't been raised among us. She jerked her attention to me—her fear for me blasting into me, weakening me further.

"Destroy them!" The harvester's deep-throated voice echoed around us, shook snow from the trees.

The hounds sprang. The Guardians fought to ward them off, stepping out, swinging their swords.

Connor was the first to make contact. The dog yelped as a gash opened across its chest, but before blood had even begun to spill out, the wound closed.

"Crap!" Connor muttered, setting his feet apart, balancing himself. "They heal."

"They're not Shifters," I said, panting, fighting to stave off the transformation. "They're immune to the effects of silver."

Gaps opened between the guardians as the hounds lured them out, nipping at them, springing at them.

A hideous scream rent through the night air. Seth!

I swung around just as his fears and horror blasted into me. Two hounds were tearing at him. His resignation encompassed me. If he didn't shift, he couldn't heal. If he shifted, the harvester would take his soul.

Lucas and Rafe fought their way to his side. Rafe

managed to thrust his sword through the heart of one of the hounds. It turned to ash.

The Guardians had split up. Half trying to protect me, the others circling Seth now that they'd chased the hounds away from him. Seth lay there, struggling to get up, desperate to rejoin the fight, but he was too weak, the blood gushing from his wounds.

He sank back to the cold snow, his gaze glazing over. His emotions swirled through me: regret, sorrow. Finally love. There was someone he loved; he'd be leaving her.

"No!"

I knew what it was to give up the one you loved more than anything. It was enough that one of us had already done it. Besides, with my ability to feel emotions, maybe my soul could overwhelm the harvester with feelings and destroy it. It seemed unlikely, but I intended to continue fighting it through eternity.

"Take me!" I yelled. "Take only me!"

I forced myself to my feet, staggered forward a few steps. Raising my arms to the sky, I called on the moon, stopped fighting the transformation, let the pain ripple through me—

The harvester solidified. Even more terrifying, its face was a mask of pain and torment. My body shimmered with the beginning of the transformation—

It reached out with those long knifelike talons—

A black streak erupted from the forest and hit the harvester with enough force to knock it down.

Daniel!

The weight of his body held the creature down. I watched in horror as it scraped its talons along Daniel's sides, creating rivulets of blood. Daniel buried his teeth into its throat, but still it fought. It bucked, yelled, and sliced into Daniel. I knew Daniel's mouth would be blistering from the heat of the creature, I knew the pain he was suffering had to be unbearable, but he refused to relinquish his hold.

Looking around frantically, I spotted Seth's sword, half buried in the snow. I lurched over to it and pulled it free.

Fighting my own pain, my own need to shift, while the others kept the hounds occupied, I lumbered over to where Daniel battled the harvester. I couldn't get to its heart from the top because Daniel was sprawled over it, striving to keep his hold on its neck. I knelt. When the harvester lifted its arm to slash at Daniel once again, I pierced its side with the sword, driving it all the way through to its heart.

A piercing cry echoed around us.

Suddenly I was swamped with emotions dancing around me, through me, quickly darting in and leaving as though I provided a passage. Love, gratitude, relief.

And I realized I was feeling what remained of all the souls the beast had harvested. With its death they were released from bondage.

A thousand souls, trapped in oblivion, providing energy to a creature that didn't deserve to exist.

I felt love so strong, so purposeful—and for the first time in my life I knew who the emotions were directed to. Daniel. These were the souls of his family, reaching out one last time. I absorbed the feeling, hoping he sensed it. If not, I'd share it with him later.

And then there was Justin. Not blaming me for realizing too late the trouble he was in. He was free now. His soul was at peace. At last.

Abruptly . . . nothingness. The souls were all gone. The emotions with them.

The harvester shrieked again, then dissolved into ash. The ash was captured on the wind and blown into oblivion. With his destruction the hounds disappeared.

Utterly exhausted, I collapsed and crawled to Daniel, tenderly touching his wounds, which were beginning to heal. "I'm sorry. I'm so sorry. Even though I can't feel your emotions, I know you. I knew you'd shift. Then it would have you, too. I couldn't bear the thought—"

Purring low in his throat, he licked my cheek.

I was aware of a shimmering in the air and glanced back to see that Seth had shifted. His wounds would heal, and whoever it was he loved—he'd return to her.

Maybe it was because Connor loved a half human/ half Shifter, loved someone who didn't shift into wolf form, that he knew what to do. He brought the quilt over and draped it over Daniel.

In the blink of an eye I was staring at Daniel's beloved face. I touched his cheek. "You should have waited to shift until you'd completely healed."

"I'll shift back soon."

"Daniel." My throat clogged; tears welled in my eyes. "How did you escape?"

"Did you think a locked door was going to hold me? I shifted and used the strength I have in panther form to beat down the door."

"You risked death by shifting." I couldn't prevent harsh scolding from creeping into my voice.

"I figured the harvester was occupied with you."

"But what if there had been more than one? What if—"

He touched my lips. "It's over, Hayden."

But I couldn't let go of what he'd risked. "I love you."

He grinned, the smile that had first made my knees grow weak. "I know. Good thing, too." He nuzzled my neck. "Because I can find you anywhere."

I was vaguely aware that we were now alone. The

Dark Guardians had left, quietly retreated. And I realized that my feelings for Daniel were so strong that there had been no room for their emotions to slip inside me. Or maybe I was becoming better at blocking what I didn't want to experience.

Then pain rippled through me. My limbs, my entire body, went numb before the nerves burst with sharp tingles. I gasped.

Daniel cradled my face between his large hands. "Hayden, do you accept me as your mate?"

"With all my heart."

He drew me close. "Concentrate on me."

His lips touched mine, hungrily, as if for the first time. Then they settled into the familiar. My body began to feel strange; I felt little undulations, as though it were preparing.

I focused on Daniel, on the feel of his arms around me, the taste of his kiss, the heat of his skin.

His emotions didn't slip inside me, but I still knew what he was feeling. He loved me. He didn't want me to suffer. He would do anything—and everything—to protect me.

I heard his purr of satisfaction, low in his throat. In animal form we'd make different sounds; we'd look different. But deep down we'd be the same.

The pain escalated, then receded as he glided his

hands over me and deepened the kiss. Passion ignited within me, drowning out everything else. Between one heartbeat and the next a thousand stars erupted within me, moonlight flowed over and through me.

When I opened my eyes, I was staring at a panther, knowing that he was staring at a wolf.

Hayden?

I'd been so afraid that, because I couldn't feel his emotions, I wouldn't be able to hear his thoughts. But they were there, whispering to me.

You're beautiful in wolf form.

I nuzzled his snout.

Are you disappointed I'm not a wolf? he asked.

Silly. Do you wish I was a panther?

I love you just the way you are.

The warmth swirled through me with his words, my heart beat harder. Even though I knew how he felt, there was satisfaction and joy in hearing the words.

I could see what remained of the wounds in his side, the long scrapes, healing quickly. The wolf in me scented them, then licked gingerly. Blood scent.

Now I'll find you anywhere, too, I thought.

The wounds healed, leaving no scars, no evidence that they'd ever been. It was our gift, our ability to heal.

What now? he asked.

I glanced at the vast white landscape spread out before

236

us. *I don't think I can run as fast as you*, I confessed.

I can adjust my stride.

I raced off, my paws kicking up snow. Daniel loped easily alongside me. No, I'd never outrun him, never escape him.

But the truth was I no longer wanted to.

TWENTY

We raced through the forest until we reached the cavern where he'd brought me the night before. As I stepped inside, my eyes adjusted to the darkness. I could see with the vision of a wolf, could see through the darkness.

What I saw surprised me.

My backpack. I wondered when he'd brought it. Sometime in the afternoon, when I was with Kayla, Lindsey, and Brittany, maybe.

I glanced back at him.

You guessed right.

You can read my thoughts even when they're not directed at you? Why can't I read yours?

Because I've learned how to hold them back. I'll teach you. So I'll know only what you want me to know.

Maybe that skill will help me hold the emotions back, too.

I could hope.

I prowled through the cavern to the area in the back where the pool was. My clothes were set on a boulder, waiting for me in human form.

You can shift in here, Daniel thought. *I'll shift in there.*

Okay. To shift, do I just think human?

Just think human.

When he was no longer visible, I closed my eyes, concentrated, felt a ripple pass through me. I opened my eyes. I was back in human form. Quickly I slipped on my jeans, my sweater, and my boots. When I walked into the front of the cavern, Daniel was standing at the entrance to the cave, staring out. Large battery-operated flashlights lit the darkness.

I took my time to study him leisurely: the broad slope of his shoulders, the length of his back. His hands were shoved into the back pockets of his jeans.

I'd almost lost this, lost him because of my fears. But it was also my fear of losing him that had given me strength to fight off my own transformation and reach down to destroy the harvester. Before Daniel I might not have fought so hard. I wouldn't have given up quietly, but neither did I have as much to lose.

I crossed over to him, slid beneath his arm. There was comfort here, familiarity.

"You're right," he said quietly. "I brought the harvester here."

"No, you didn't."

He looked down at me, his eyes questioning, wanting to believe my words.

"You've been here since the summer. If it had followed you, it would have shown up sooner," I said.

"I want to believe that."

"I do believe it. We don't know everything about the harvester. It's not as if it's been on *Oprah*. We don't know why it was dormant for centuries. We don't know why it made its appearance now. I do know it was the one that killed your parents. I felt their souls. They love you so much."

Tears welled in his eyes and he blinked them back. "Are they at peace?"

"They are now, yes."

"I don't know how it found my family. I don't know how many more of my kind it might have killed. Like I told you, we're not like the wolves. We don't stay in packs." He looked down at me. "I'd like to go in search of the others. Let them know about this place. We're loners, you and I, but we belong together." He touched my cheek. "But I won't go if you want to stay here. And if the elders will let me stay. You mean more to me than anything."

Before I could respond or give him an answer, he took me in his arms and kissed me. I thought I'd never have this again. Now here it was.

He was willing to give up what he wanted to do because he wanted me more. But I cared enough about him to be willing not to let him give up what he wanted to do.

I'd often felt love—coming from others, directed toward others. The love of a parent for a child, a friend for a friend, and with Connor, the love of a lover for a lover. In all cases love was a strong emotion, not easily contained once it was unleashed. I realized now that love was like a blossoming flower that continually added more and more petals. But there was no end point. There was no full bloom. It went on forever. Growing, strengthening.

I hadn't known Daniel long, but I knew in my heart that he was my true mate.

When he drew back, he touched my cheek, just as he had that afternoon behind the chocolate shop. His touch was warm, his eyes sincere. I didn't have to feel his emotions to know their depth.

"I love you, Hayden," he said.

I went back into his arms, pressed my face to his chest, heard the thundering of his heart. "I love you, too."

He took my hand and led me outside. We sat on a snow-covered boulder and watched as the moon began its descent. I thought I should have felt cold, but with Daniel's arm around me, I was warm. Happy. Madly in love.

TWENTY-ONE

Returning to Wolford the next morning was not the joyous occasion that I'd expected. The elders and the Dark Guardians weren't exactly happy with Daniel.

Yes, he'd quite possibly saved all of our butts with his attack on the harvester. But there was the little matter of his not being completely honest about himself.

So two minutes after we walked through the front door, he was standing in front of them in the council room. The elders were sitting at a table studying him as though he was an exotic creature—which I guessed he was.

On either end of their table was another table at an

angle, and the Dark Guardians filled each one. I sat at the end of one of the tables. Now that I'd experienced my shift, I was a member of this elite group.

While there was a chance that Daniel was about to be kicked out of it.

He stood tall, straight, and proud, his shoulders back, his head high. I felt so much pride. That magnificent guy was mine.

Finally Elder Wilde cleared his throat and said, "You came here under false pretenses, Mr. Foster."

I saw Daniel flinch, and I understood why. Before last night they would have called him Guardian Foster. They'd essentially stripped him of his place, were announcing that he wasn't one of them. I knew there was a time when he wouldn't have been bothered by the change. When he was a complete loner, when he didn't know what it was to truly belong.

"I told you I came here to serve as a Dark Guardian," he stated flatly.

"You neglected to tell us that you shifted into panther rather than wolf form," Elder Wilde reminded him.

"I didn't see that what I shifted into affected my ability to do my job." He glanced down, then lifted his glittering green gaze to them. "And okay, yes, I didn't think you'd accept me if you knew I was of the panther clan."

"How many panthers are there?" Lucas asked. He

ignored his grandfather's stern look.

"I don't know," Daniel said. "We don't keep track of our members the way you do. It's one of our weaknesses."

"And you didn't think we needed to know that the harvester murdered your parents?" Elder Thomas asked, putting the inquisition back on course.

"I didn't know what killed them until the night Justin died. And then all I could think about was protecting Hayden."

My heart went out to him. He looked over at me, and I did everything in my power to convey that, no matter what happened, I stood behind him. Then finally he continued, "I thought if I told you everything you'd be hesitant to accept me. I needed to learn what you know so I can save my clan from extinction. Maybe part of the lesson for me was that I needed to learn to trust those who aren't like me. What I did I did out of concern for my own species. I was putting what I thought were their needs first. I know now that I have to put all Shifters first, not just my species. What we shift into doesn't define us. I can't undo what I've done in the past, but I can swear to you that you will never find a more dedicated Dark Guardian for your kind."

"Perhaps," Elder Wilde said thoughtfully, "the first step is not to view us as a *kind* separate from yours. As you said, we are all Shifters. That is our common bond.

Just as there are some Shifters with empathic abilities and some without. We don't separate them out; we don't see them as not belonging with us." He glanced over at me. "Would you agree, Hayden?"

I nodded. "I do."

Elder Wilde gazed around the table, then he looked at Daniel. "You are welcome to stay among us, Guardian Foster."

Relief swamped me, and I couldn't prevent a small smile from forming on my lips.

"Thank you, elders, Dark Guardians. Because you have offered to let me stay, I can now leave with a light heart."

"You intend to leave?" Elder Wilde asked.

"Yes, sir. There are many like me who are lost, who don't know what we as Shifters can be. Who hide what they are and have no place to celebrate it. I want them to know that they're not alone."

"Then you do so with our blessing, and we look forward to welcoming them here as well."

"Thank you."

I shoved my chair back, stood, walked over to Daniel, and slipped my hand into his. "He's my mate. I'm going with him. I'd like your blessing, too. But I'll leave without it if I have to."

"You have our blessing," Elder Wilde said. "And if

your parents were here with us now, I think you would have theirs as well. They wanted nothing more than for you to be happy."

"I can promise you that she will be," Daniel said. He squeezed my hand, then put his arm around me, drawing me in close to his side, right where I belonged. Next to his heart.

At the top of Daniel's tattoo where the knots had once ended, he had another tattoo embedded beneath his skin: a Celtic symbol representing my name. He said the tattoo that began on his bicep and went up over his back represented his journey from being separate to being included. It was the story of my journey as well.

With Daniel at my side, often distracting me, I was able to be out among the other Shifters. Only the most intense of emotions ever invaded me now. I was learning to use them to signal when someone needed help. I still didn't consider this ability a gift. But I was accepting that maybe it wasn't exactly a curse.

"You'll be back in time for the summer solstice, right?" Kayla asked as she wrapped her arms around me.

Daniel and I were heading out to search for other Shifters like him. I wasn't certain how much help I'd be since I couldn't sense their emotions, but for me there would be peace in that.

"We'll try," I said. We were standing in the front yard at Wolford saying good-bye to everyone.

We were going to travel on the snowmobile, a gift from the elders. I didn't know if it would be as exciting to ride on it now that it was sanctioned. We were still a month or so away from the spring thaws, but Daniel was anxious to get started.

I hugged everyone, saving Elder Wilde for last. I was surprised when tears stung my eyes as his arms came around me. He'd always seemed so strong, but suddenly he felt so frail.

"Travel safely, Hayden," he said. "And remember, this is your home."

"It is," I acknowledged to him, and probably for the first time in my life to myself.

I climbed on the snowmobile behind Daniel.

"Ready?" he asked.

"Ready."

He took off, and excitement spurred through me. I didn't know what we'd find out there.

At the top of a rise Daniel brought the snowmobile to a halt, and we glanced back at Wolford.

"We don't have to go," he said.

I shook my head. "No, I think we do. We have other enemies. If the harvester found us, maybe they will, too. We should tell other Shifters about Wolford, those from your clan and anyone else, so they'll have a safe haven."

"We'll come back," he promised.

I tightened my hold on him. "I know."

He revved the engine and we glided over the snow, the wind rushing by us. I was lost in a world where I felt only my own emotions.

Happiness. Joy. Anticipation. Love.

Daniel.